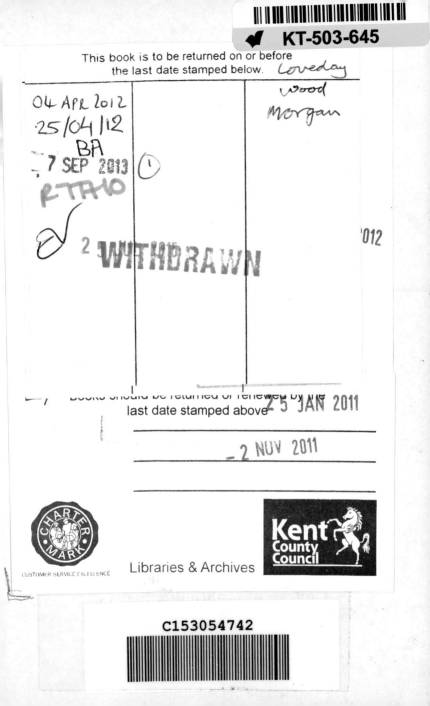

EACH TIME WE MEET

Sarah's new hairdressing salon gives a much-needed boost to her life away from her overbearing ex-boyfriend. Then, she meets Alice, her neighbour — sometimes strange and moody, but also sweet and generous — and is later introduced to her husband, Dr Gareth Bradley. But all is not what it seems, and when Sarah realises she is attracted to Gareth, she discovers how devious Alice can be. Throughout that hot summer of 1955, fear and tension builds within everyone — especially the dedicated, overworked doctor . . .

*Books by Marlene E. McFadden
in the Linford Romance Library:*

PATH OF TRUE LOVE
TOMORROW ALWAYS COMES
WHEN LOVE IS LOST

MARLENE E. McFADDEN

EACH TIME WE MEET

Complete and Unabridged

LINFORD
Leicester

First published in Great Britain in 2006

First Linford Edition
published 2007

British Library CIP Data

McFadden, Marlene E. (Marlene Elizabeth),
1937 –
    Each time we meet.—Large print ed.—
Linford romance library
    1. Love stories
    2. Large type books
    I. Title
    823.9'14 [F]

    ISBN 978-1-84617-682-1

Published by
F. A. Thorpe (Publishing)
Anstey, Leicestershire
Set by Words & Graphics Ltd.
Anstey, Leicestershire
Printed and bound in Great Britain by
T. J. International Ltd., Padstow, Cornwall

This book is printed on acid-free paper

1

The shop bell jangled and Sarah turned and saw who had come in. 'I'm Alice,' the young woman said, holding out her hand. 'Alice Bradley. I live next door.'

Sarah shook hands. 'Yes, I know,' she said, smiling. 'I've seen you. I'm Sarah Mallinson.'

Close up, Alice seemed even thinner than she had when Sarah had looked out of her sitting-room window above the salon and noticed her neighbour crossing the wide expanse of lawn to the summer house. Dressed all in white with her long, pale hair loose about her shoulders she had seemed to Sarah to be almost ethereal. When she had gone into the summerhouse and laid out on a chaise longue, trailing her slender fingers on to the floor, the name *Ophelia* had sprung to Sarah's mind.

Now she could see that Alice Bradley

was older than the seventeen or eighteen years she had imagined — more like her own age of twenty-four. It was only her mannerisms, her child-like smile, the way she stood rocking on her heels with her hands clasped behind her back that made her appear so much younger. The pale blue eyes were definitely older, staring, taking everything in.

'You've redecorated,' she stated.

'Yes,' Sarah glanced around at her handiwork. 'Just a facelift.'

'I like the colour. It's fresh and summery.'

'Did Ginny Taylor do your hair?' Sarah asked.

If she had, Sarah couldn't help thinking rather unkindly that she hadn't made such a good job of it, the ends of Alice's fine hair were raggedy, uneven, her fringe much too long.

Alice laughed. 'Oh, no, I haven't been to a hairdresser in ages.' She touched her hair, but not with any self-consciousness. 'You see, when I was fourteen I had rheumatic fever. I nearly died and the doctor advised that I have my hair cropped, to conserve my strength, he said. I was very ill, but that didn't stop me from becoming very upset at losing all my lovely hair. It was much longer then, much thicker too. I vowed I wouldn't have it cut again, but . . . I don't know,' she shrugged her thin shoulders, 'it doesn't seem to grow very much. That's why I've come. I thought you could do something with it. Not crop it, of course,' she shuddered at the thought, 'just make it look less of a mess.'

'Well . . . ' Sarah began carefully, 'I don't officially open till tomorrow. I just came down here to bring some towels and have a final look around.'

Alice's pale eyes seemed to narrow. For a few seconds she looked intensely annoyed. Then she said sweetly, 'Oh, please. I'm not very good at being with people so I won't come near after today. I looked through the window and saw you were alone. I can pay,' she thrust her hand into the patch pocket of her white dress and produced a small pink purse.

Sarah gave in. Alice had a definite endearing quality that was difficult to resist. 'All right,' she said, reaching out to a pile of fresh white towels. 'Do you want me to wash your hair first?'

'Do you think you should?' Alice asked, moving and sitting in the chair before the washbasin and mirror.

'I think it's best.'

Alice grinned. 'All right.'

She folded her hands in her lap and stared through the mirror at Sarah.

So, Sarah thought, I have my first customer. Not the first person whose hair she had done, of course, she had been a qualified stylist for four years, but the first in this new salon, owned entirely by herself. Only half an hour ago she had stood looking around the sitting-room of her small flat above the salon.

'A new home, a new business, a new life,' she had thought. The past was

4

behind her now and she had only the future to look forward to.

As her eyes met Alice's through the mirror, Alice suddenly said, 'You were watching me, weren't you?'

Sarah was a little taken aback by the direct question. 'Well . . . I saw you in your garden, yes,' she admitted.

Alice shook her head. 'No. You were spying on me, standing behind your curtain. You stood there for some time. Even when I went into the summer-house you remained there. Watching me.'

Sarah gave a nervous laugh. She found this young woman distinctly unnerving. 'I'm sorry,' was all she could think of to say. 'But my sitting-room window overlooks your back garden. What can I do about it?'

With one of her quick changes of mood, Alice smiled beautifully. 'You can't do anything, of course,' she declared. 'I shall just have to be more careful. Not sit around in my bathing costume or anything like that. I spend a lot of time in the summerhouse, actually. I have to rest often. Gareth insists on it. My rheumatic fever left me with a weak heart, you see.'

'I'm sorry,' Sarah said again. Then, as she flicked her fingers through Alice's silky hair, 'Is Gareth your husband?'

Alice paused fractionally lowering her eyes, before glancing once again at Sarah through the mirror. 'That's right,' she said. 'I'm the doctor's wife. Not a very good advertisement, am I?' She laughed delightedly.

For the next few minutes whilst Sarah washed Alice's hair they didn't speak. Sarah was thinking about her new neighbours, not only Alice, but her husband, the doctor. She had known there was a doctor's surgery next door; she had read the plaque on the wall the day she moved in.

Dr Gareth Bradley, followed by a string of letters, setting out his qualifications. She had pictured in her mind a middle-aged man in a tweed jacket, smelling faintly of pipe smoke.

When Sarah first came to look at the salon, she had been impressed by its position; a crossroads, in a small, rural suburb of the large industrial town of Heaton. Behind the pretty red-roofed bungalows, the old church and grave-yard, and the local pub called The Bell, fields and hills seemed to stretch as far as the eye could see, but the suburb itself, known as Fenton, was quite thriving, and a bus route ran through it, descending a steep hill to the village of Thorley.

Sarah had instinctively felt she could start her new life here and be happy. She swamped Alice's wet hair in a huge towel. When Alice emerged she contin-ued their previous conversation, as though there had been no break.

'Of course, there was no problem when Ginny Taylor owned the salon. She didn't live in the flat. I expect it was a bit of a mess, wasn't it?'

'Not too bad, a bit neglected perhaps,' Sarah said. 'A lick of paint here and there and a good clean did the trick.'

'May I come and look inside?' Alice asked.

'Yes, if you want to.' Sarah stroked her comb through Alice's hair. 'Now, shall I trim your fringe quite drastically?' she suggested.

Alice smiled. 'I'm in your hands,' she declared.

Sarah set to work, a little nervously, which was ridiculous as she knew her job and had never had any complaints. But then, she had never had a customer quite like Alice Bradley before.

'What do you think of our house?' Alice asked next.

'It's beautiful,' Sarah told her.

'We came here four years ago. In 1951. Like your flat, The White House,' she paused and grinned, 'yes, believe it or not that's what it's called, needed a great deal of tender, loving care. Gareth was taking up his first general practice, you see. He was determined to be a family doctor, he thoroughly approved

8

of the National Health Scheme. He could have done so much better, and certainly made more money if he'd gone into the private sector, but that wouldn't have suited Gareth's pioneering spirit at all.

'He was at university when the war started, and later he worked with the Ministry of Health, and he was like an excited schoolboy when he first got the keys to The White House . . . So, here we are, and I'm the doctor's perfect little wife, except when I'm feeling ill and can't drag one foot in front of the other, mooning around pale as a ghost. I'm sure Gareth's patients get put off. If he can't cure his own wife, where's the hope for them?'

It was quite an outburst. Sarah could have pointed out that Dr Bradley wouldn't have been able to practise medicine on his own wife, but that would have sounded pretentious and, of course, Alice would know that for herself.

She snipped at her customer's hair.

With yet another swing of mood Alice smiled into the mirror.

'I say,' she cried, 'that looks really good!'

'Do you think so?'' Sarah was pleased.

'I do.'

Alice's thin, pale face seemed rounder, fuller and the short fringe brought out the blue of her large eyes. 'How much do I owe you?' she asked.

Sarah told her and she took out the money, counting it carefully into Sarah's palm, like a child, every last penny.

'I'm so grateful, Sarah,' she said, eyeing herself in the mirror. 'Gareth is going to be amazed when he sees me.' She walked towards the door then paused before turning to face Sarah again. 'Come to tea this afternoon,' she declared. 'Gareth is usually free about four o'clock, unless there's an emergency, and I'm sure there won't be. I want him to meet my new friend.'

Were they friends? Sarah wasn't all

that sure she wanted Alice Bradley for a friend.

'All right,' she said. 'I'll come round about four if you're sure that's all right.'

'Perfect!' Alice said, and was gone.

Alice answered Sarah's ring of the door bell. There were two bells, one which stated, *Night Emergencies only*. Sarah thought sympathetically about Dr Bradley perhaps having to be woken from sleep should a patient need him in the middle of the night. But that was all part and parcel of the life of a general practitioner she supposed.

Alice was wearing lipstick and a hint of rouge which seemed to make her look less pale and wan. She flicked her hair for Sarah's approval.

'Come in,' she invited. 'Gareth's not here yet so I'm afraid you'll be here when he first sees the new me.'

Sarah entered a large square hall with a turned staircase to the right and white painted doors to either side. The carpet was a dark elegant red and gold. Alice ushered her into a room on the left. A

11

bright, sunny room, pleasantly and comfortably furnished. In front of the fireplace with its display of dried flowers stood a small round table, positively groaning under the weight of cakes and scones and a delicate white and gold tea set.

'My, this is a surprise,' Sarah said, suddenly realising she was quite hungry, having skipped lunch.

'I wish I could say it was all my own work,' Alice said wistfully, 'but I can't even boil an egg. Mrs Harmon, our housekeeper, made the cakes and things.' She indicated a chair and Sarah sat down. Alice sat opposite her, curling her slim legs under her full yellow cotton skirt.

'Would you like to be mother?' Alice asked pleasantly.

Sarah didn't mind but thought it an odd request. She passed Alice a cup of tea. It was far weaker than she preferred it, making her wonder how much tea Mrs Harmon had sprinkled into the pot.

'Help yourself,' Alice invited. 'Mrs Harmon makes wonderful cakes and pastries. It's much easier now rationing's finally at an end I suppose.'

Sarah chose a slice of fruit cake and took a nibble. It was delicious. 'Aren't you eating?' she asked.

'I'm not hungry,' Alice told her.

Sarah could have said, 'You look like you need fattening up,' but didn't.

'Don't worry,' Alice went on, 'when Gareth gets here he'll clear the table. He has an enormous appetite.'

Sarah felt self-conscious eating when her hostess wasn't and consequently, though she eyed the scones enviously, she limited herself to the one slice of fruit cake. Alice was urging her to at least try the Victoria sponge cake when the door opened and Dr Bradley came in.

At least, Sarah presumed it was the doctor. He was nothing like her imaginary vision. He was nowhere near middle age for one thing, taller and more handsome with not a touch of tweed in sight. His hair was dark brown, swept back from his forehead.

He was wearing a dark blue suit with a white shirt, but his dark tie was knotted loosely at his throat as though, Sarah thought, he had pulled it that way as he came through the door. He looked startled when he saw her.

'Oh, I'm sorry, I didn't know you had company,' he said, smiling in a friendly way at Sarah.

Alice jumped up, crossing to her husband and kissing him on the cheek. 'Gareth, this is Sarah, she's taken over Ginny Taylor's salon next door.'

'Hello, Sarah,' Dr Bradley held out his hand. His handshake was firm. The next minute he had swung round to face Alice.

'My goodness, your hair!' he cried.

Alice pirouetted before him. 'Do you like it?' she asked like an excited child showing off a party dress.

'It's . . . very nice, but was it wise, Alice, having it cut? I presume you went to the salon. Didn't we agree you wouldn't go out today, not after . . . '

Alice broke in, anger flaring rapidly in her blue eyes. 'You agreed, you mean,' she snapped. 'I'm all right, Gareth. I wish you wouldn't fuss so.'

He remained perfectly calm, whilst Sarah sat there feeling embarrassed. 'I'm concerned about you, dear,' he said.

'Well, don't be.' Alice sat down abruptly again, composing herself, smiling sweetly at Sarah. 'Isn't he beastly, Sarah? And very rude too.'

Dr Bradley moved towards Sarah, apology in his dark eyes. 'I'm sorry, Sarah, please forgive me.' He sat down beside her on the sofa. 'Is there any tea left in that pot?' he asked, reaching for a piece of the sponge cake.

She was acutely aware how close he was beside her on the sofa. In fact, when their fingers touched accidentally as they both reached for the tea pot at the same time, she felt a definite shiver of excitement running through her.

Don't be ridiculous, she scolded herself silently, and edged slightly away from him on the sofa. The tea party progressed without any further outburst from Alice. In fact, she was quite chatty and friendly, asking Sarah about herself, whilst her husband put in the odd remark of his own.

Sarah was careful what she told them. It was enough for them to know that she had moved to Fenton from the other side of the main town, that she was the only child of an elderly mother and had trained as a hairdresser under one of Heaton's most celebrated stylists. The rest was her business; she would not expect to probe into the Bradley's private lives and was sure they would respect her own privacy.

At least, she was sure Gareth would. She could never be certain how Alice would react or how directly she might question.

It was perhaps some ten minutes after Gareth's arrival that Alice suddenly leaned back in her chair, closing her eyes and sighing deeply. Immediately Gareth rose and crossed to her.

'What is it, Alice?' he asked sharply.

'I suddenly feel very tired,' she murmured.

'Perhaps you'd better go and lie down for a while,' Gareth suggested.

Without opening her eyes, Alice said, 'Ever the attentive doctor,' but she allowed her husband to help her to her feet, smiling apologetically at Sarah. 'Please excuse me, Sarah,' she said, 'and thank you for cutting my hair.'

'My pleasure,' Sarah told her.

As they left the room, Alice leaning heavily on Gareth, he turned to Sarah and said, 'Please don't go yet, Sarah. Not till I come downstairs.'

So she sat alone and took the opportunity to pick up one of the tempting-looking scones. It tasted as delicious as it looked. Gareth returned some minutes later.

'I'm sorry if I overtaxed Alice by cutting her hair,' Sarah said. 'She did mention to me that she had a weak heart, but she was most insistent.'

Gareth smiled a weary smile. 'Alice is

always most insistent at getting her own way and getting round people,' he said. He reached forward and touched the tea pot. 'Shall I ask Mrs Harmon to make some more tea?' he suggested.

'Oh, no, not on my behalf.' Sarah got to her feet. 'I think I'd better go. I've a hundred and one things I should do before I open the salon tomorrow.'

They stood facing one another. Gareth had removed the jacket of his suit and had his hands in his trouser pockets. Once again, Sarah was struck by an intense feeling of suppressed excitement.

'May I wish you luck for your new venture?' he said.

'Thank you,' she murmured.

'And, do please come again.'

'Will that be all right?' She wasn't sure she wanted to come again. She didn't know if she could trust her feelings for this man. She felt annoyed with herself. This was a fine start to a new life, reacting like a schoolgirl to the first man she met, and a married man at that!

'I think you might be good for Alice,' Gareth said. 'She doesn't have any real friends, her illness keeps her housebound most of the time. If you could make the time to be . . . nice to her I would be most grateful. Of course, I know you must have your own busy life to lead, and I have absolutely no right to ask you to get involved in ours.'

His expression was so concerned that Sarah heard herself saying. 'What are neighbours for?'

Whereupon Gareth's tense features seemed to relax. 'Thank you,' he breathed. 'Let me show you to the door.'

He shook hands with her again, holding on to her fingers for what seemed like a long time. When she reached the gate she turned; Gareth was still standing in the doorway, watching her.

2

Sarah quickly found that her appointment book was filling up nicely. The salon was in a good position, midway between the town centre and the village of Thorley and on a main bus route. In fact by the end of the first week, Sarah was seriously considering advertising for a junior to come along as an apprentice hair stylist.

At the end of her working day she was so tired she usually went straight up to the flat, had a long soak in the bath and a fairly early night, despite it being early summer and light until late. She had not seen either Alice or Gareth since that first day. Or more accurately she had not spoken to them.

She had seen Gareth a few times, leaving the surgery with his medical bag, probably making his rounds. She was sure he never noticed her and was very careful not to stand too obviously at her sitting-room window especially when Alice ventured out into the garden which she seemed to do most days. Sarah could often see her, apparently lying asleep on the chaise longue in the summerhouse.

She felt sorry for Alice. It must be frustrating for her being a semi-invalid with nothing to do all day but lie around. Surely she must get bored. Sarah had never seen her reading a book, for instance, or even admiring the flowers in the garden, only walking languidly towards the summerhouse and taking up her position on the chaise longue.

Sarah did not know whether to go round and ring the doorbell or to wait for a specific invitation to the house. She considered inviting Alice to her flat. She had, after all, expressed a wish to see inside, but there were a lot of steps to climb and she didn't know whether Alice would be up to it.

It was on her second Sunday at the

flat, just after breakfast, a leisurely weekend affair when Sarah had been able to read the Sunday papers and laze around in her dressing gown, that she heard the loud and desperate knocking on the street door. She kept that door locked and this was the first time anyone had come to the flat.

She opened the door. Alice dashed inside, out of breath.

'Oh, Sarah, I can't bear it,' she cried, collapsing into Sarah's surprised arms.

'What's the matter?' Sarah asked.

'Let's go up to your flat,' Alice begged.

Sarah helped her up the steep flight of steps. Once in the sitting-room Alice flung herself on to the sofa, hiding her face in a cushion.

'Are you all right?' Sarah asked in a worried voice. 'Can I get you some tea? Or a drink of water?'

'No, no, I'm all right.'

But she wasn't. She was breathing heavily, her thin shoulders heaving. Should she insist on fetching Gareth,

Sarah wondered?

Alice was wearing a long-skirted pale pink dress with a stand-up collar. Even at nine o'clock in the morning she was well-dressed, making Sarah acutely conscious of her old dressing gown that should not have been seen by any eyes but her own, and she couldn't help wondering how a semi-invalid like Alice, could find the energy to be so well turned out at that hour on a Sunday morning.

Alice suddenly sat up straight. 'We're having a visitor,' she declared. 'She's coming to stay indefinitely. A ten-year-old girl! Can you imagine that? A child running about the house, making a noise, getting in the way.'

'A relative?' Sarah ventured when Alice didn't seem prepared to tell her anymore.

'Sort of. A cousin. Well, the child of Gareth's cousin, Edith. Edith's a widow. She's had a rough life, I'm not saying she hasn't. Married the wrong man who treated her abominably, then died of a heart attack when Audrey, the little girl, was six. They live in Leeds and we never see them, but there's no-one else. No other relative who can help out, and Edith must have had Gareth's name and address when they took her into hospital.'

She was talking very fast and was completely wound up.

'Your cousin is ill?' Sarah asked.

Alice gave her a sharp look. 'Not my cousin. Gareth's. Oh, yes, had a nervous breakdown and the authorities, who incidentally could quite easily put young Audrey into a children's home, should they chose to do so, have asked if Gareth would look after her. Well, Gareth, the knight in shining armour, has told them yes, of course he will and he's picking her up from Leeds this afternoon.

'Mrs Harmon's running around like a headless chicken getting a room prepared for her, silly woman. Well, she has four children of her own so will take it all in her stride, I suppose, but I don't want a child about the place, Sarah. I'm not well myself, you know that.'

Alice was showing scant sympathy for the little girl, Sarah thought, but she had a point. Would she be up to coping with this Audrey? On the other hand, she could understand Gareth's point of view. He could hardly refuse to be her guardian and have her put in a home.

'Let me put the kettle on,' she said, unable to think of anything more constructive to say.

As she moved towards the tiny kitchenette she heard footsteps coming up the stairs from the street and after a brief knock at the door, Gareth put his head round.

'Is Alice here?' he asked.

'Yes, she is,' Sarah told him, self-consciously pulling her dressing gown closer around her.

Gareth came in and shut the door. Today he was more casually dressed in a pair of brown corduroy trousers and a dark checked shirt. He looked slightly harassed as well he might, but no less handsome and once again Sarah felt that little thrill rippling through her.

'The street door was slightly open so I came straight in, I hope you don't mind,' Gareth said.

'Not at all,' Sarah said. 'I was just going to make some tea. Would you like some?'

Gareth grinned. 'Just what the doctor ordered,' he remarked.

She showed him where Alice was and when she went back in the sitting-room a few minutes later, they were arguing hotly. Alice had got up and was pacing up and down, Gareth urging her to calm down.

'How can I calm down?' she threw at him. 'How can you do this to me, Gareth?'

'For once in your life try to think about someone other than yourself.' Gareth's voice was calm.

'But we hardly know Edith and we wouldn't recognise this Audrey if we passed her in the street. Why can't you allow the authorities to do what they get paid for?'

'Because Edith and Audrey are flesh and blood and they need our help. I don't want to argue any more about it. It's going to happen, Alice, and you may as well get used to it.

Sarah half-expected Alice to throw at him, 'They're not my flesh and blood,' but she didn't.

'Tea!' she announced brightly, trying to defuse the situation.

She had no idea how she had landed up in the middle of all this. Was it to become a habit, Alice running to her on a daily basis with moans about little Audrey, using her as a shoulder to cry on?

They managed to remain fairly civilised as they accepted cups of tea and sipped them quietly. Then Gareth stood up.

'Thanks for the tea, Sarah,' he said, 'come on, Alice, let's go home.'

With a great sigh she got to her feet and strolled towards the door, turning to Sarah to say, 'The next time you see me I'll have a little brat in tow, I suppose.'

Sarah chose to ignore the remark and so did Gareth, but Sarah could see he was annoyed with his wife and wondered if the bitter arguing would continue when they got back home.

The rest of the day passed fairly quietly, but well on into Sunday evening, whilst Sarah was listening to a musical concert on the wireless, once again someone knocked on the street door.

'Oh, no,' she thought, 'not Alice again,' and wondered whether to pretend she was out, but knowing Alice she would have looked up and seen the lights on and Sarah didn't feel she could meet her neighbour's recriminations the next time she saw her, so she went downstairs.

Of course, Audrey would now be at The White House and Alice, being Alice, would want to share her moans with what she assumed was a sympathetic ear.

But it was Gareth, not Alice, who stood on the doorstop. He shrugged his shoulders when he saw her and gave a sheepish grin which made him appear very boyish and vulnerable.

'Me again!' Were his first words. 'I expect you're sick of the sight of us Bradleys.'

Sarah would never, she was sure, be sick of the sight of Dr Gareth Bradley, married man or no married man.

'Come in,' she told him.

It was the first time, Sarah realised, that she had really been alone with Gareth and she prayed Alice would not appear and spoil the moment.

'I felt that perhaps I owed you an apology and some explanation about what's going on,' Gareth began. 'Alice should not have come round here like she did, getting into a state and involving you in it, but then I'm afraid, that's Alice. Very highly strung. I think it's because when she was a young girl she was quite ill and everyone more or less indulged her.

She had overheard her doctor say she must not be upset under any circumstances and she played on that. Still is playing on it, really.'

'How ill is she, Gareth?' Sarah asked.

'Well, her heart is none too strong and sometimes she does have very bad days, but she has good days too, and it's on these good days that we try to encourage her to be more active, but Alice, being the perverse creature she is, always wants to push herself when she shouldn't, like coming to you to have her hair cut the day after she was really bad and confined to her bed, and do absolutely nothing but mope when she could be more active.

'Oh, dear, here I go burdening you with our troubles. I'm no better than Alice, am I? But you're such a nice person and it's good, like now, to get out of the house for a few minutes sanity. Finally I've got young Audrey to bed and to sleep and believe me that was quite a struggle. The poor child is bewildered, dumped on virtual strangers like she is, missing her mother, very scared. Of course, I know young children are very adaptable and I have hopes that Audrey will settle down given time and patience.'

'And your cousin? How is she?'

Gareth looked at her gravely. 'Not good, I'm afraid. She's in a psychiatric wing. A long term patient, it seems. So, Audrey will be part of our family for some time to come.'

'And Alice?' Sarah ventured.

'Also sleeping at the moment. She's taken a sedative and should sleep till morning.' He gave her one of his boyish smiles. 'Come the dawn? Well, we'll just have to brace ourselves and wait and see.'

Then to Sarah's surprise Gareth reached out and took hold of her hand, patting her fingers gently. She held her breath waiting for him to say something, not knowing whether to leave her hand where it was or snatch it away hurriedly.

'Thank you, Sarah,' he said softly, 'for

just being there. It may sound corny but I feel like I've known you for ages.'

She felt the same, but now she wriggled uncomfortably, desperately seeking for the right words to say. Not wishing to make too much of what could only be a friendly gesture on Gareth's part.

But when he leaned forward and kissed her on the lips she did pull free, the spell broken, leaping upwards.

'I think you'd better leave,' she said.

Gareth got up too. 'I . . . I'm sorry, I shouldn't have done that, but I thought . . . ' his voice trailed off.

'Yes, what did you think, Dr Bradley?' Sarah was trembling, but trying to keep her voice steady.

He hung his head. 'I don't know. Forgive me,' and he walked past her and out of the room.

She heard his footsteps descending the stairs and the street door opening and closing. She sat down abruptly, and her shaking fingers touched gently where Gareth's lips had been. Such a little kiss, so gentle, so . . . inoffensive and so unforgivable as he was not only married, but a doctor as well.

And now she would have to try to avoid him, but wouldn't that be difficult? Alice seemed to regard her as a friend, perhaps an only friend and there was the child. They were living practically on top of one another.

Oh, dear, not another emotional tangle from which there was never an escape. Most likely the kiss had meant nothing at all; perhaps she was reading far too much into it, but she had to be honest with herself. On her part the moment had been far from nothing. She hadn't expected it, she had certainly never encouraged it, but it had happened. The holding of her hand; the kiss.

Two things that could never be undone.

3

At half-past eight the next morning, just as Sarah was about to open up the salon to prepare for her first appointment at nine, she heard someone screaming. Loud, ear piercing screams and a distressed voice yelling out, 'No, no, let me go!'

It was coming from The White House.

She ran round the corner on to the main road and saw Gareth on his drive, attempting to drag a young child down towards his parked car. It could only be Audrey and she was clinging with all her might to the door frame. When Gareth managed to extract one hand from the frame, the other took over. To say he looked harassed was an understatement and the child herself was in a terrible state. Hair untidy, mouth open wide as she screamed, and tears running down her face.

Sarah started up the drive, uncertain at that point if she could be of any help, but willing to try. Gareth saw her and called out, 'Sarah, I'm at my wits' end with this young lady.'

'What's the matter?' Sarah spoke loudly to try to top Audrey's screams which only seemed to have got worse with Sarah's arrival.

'Believe it or not I'm trying to get her to school.' Gareth sighed.

'Don't want to go to school,' Audrey wailed. 'I won't go. I want my mummy.'

Audrey would have been a very pretty little girl, Sarah decided, were it not for her red, weeping eyes and her anger and terror. She was wearing a blue and white checked dress with a little white collar and someone had attempted to tie a white ribbon in her short brown hair, but this had come undone and was trailing down the side of her tear-streaked face. The navy blue cardigan she wore was hanging off one shoulder.

'She can't go to school like that,' Sarah said.

'She has to, it's the law. I've already spoken to the headmaster and he's expecting her. There are a few weeks yet to the summer holidays and Audrey can't miss all that schooling.'

'Does she have to start today particularly?' Sarah asked, aware that a couple of women were standing outside the church watching the proceedings with avid interest.

'What else am I going to with her?' Gareth yelled. 'I've got a nine o'clock surgery and then my rounds.' He bent his head to speak directly to the child over whom he towered. 'Now, come on, Audrey, be a good girl.'

But Audrey was having none of it. She stamped her foot, she wriggled, she tried to yank free. 'I don't want to go, I don't want to go,' she sobbed.

'Can't Alice watch her for a few hours?' Sarah suggested.

Gareth glared at her. 'You are joking, of course. Alice is still in bed. She refuses to get out of bed until Audrey is safely at school. She says evenings and weekends will be as much as she can stand. And Mrs Harmon can't help either. She's not coming in till this afternoon. She's taking her husband to hospital.'

'Then I'll look after her.' Sarah was amazed to hear herself saying those words. What on earth was she going to do with a ten-year-old child in the salon all day? Especially one who was likely to scream blue murder all the time.

Gareth looked sorely tempted, then he shook his head. 'No, I can't give into her like that. It will only start all over again tomorrow morning.'

'Not necessarily,' Sarah pointed out. 'You've got to give her time. Hasn't she got enough on her plate, adjusting to being with you and Alice, away from her mother, without having to face school as well?'

Sarah could well remember her first day at school. She, too, had cried and refused to go. Not that it had done her any good, of course, but she hadn't just been wrenched away from her mother and left with a man and woman she didn't know.

Sarah crouched down before Audrey who miraculously stopped crying as if by magic and after staring at Sarah for a long moment, suddenly turned her face into Gareth's side and put her arms around him.

'Well, I never!' Gareth cried.

'Audrey, would you like to stay with me and not go to school today?' Sarah asked. 'Just for today. Mind you, you'll have to go tomorrow. If you promise to be a good girl you can come into my hairdressing shop and help me.'

Audrey revealed half her face and mumbled, 'What, cut people's hair, you mean?'

Sarah smiled. 'No, not exactly, but you can still help me. Sweep the floor, fold the towels, things like that.'

After a short silence Audrey nodded vigorously. 'Yes,' she said.

'You will?' Sarah made herself sound

thrilled as though Audrey was doing her a big favour.

The child's face lit up in a beatific smile. 'Yes, please,' she said.

Gareth heaved a great sigh of relief. 'Sarah,' he said, 'you've saved my life.'

Sarah stood up straight. 'Don't mention it,' she said.

They looked into each other's eyes, then Sarah looked away quickly, remembering the previous evening. Gareth coughed in an embarrassed way and Sarah knew he was remembering it too. She held out her hand to Audrey.

'Come along then, Audrey,' she said, 'we've got things to do.'

Without hesitation the child put her small hand into Sarah's.

'Thanks, Sarah!' Gareth called out as she and Audrey walked down the drive.

At four o'clock, Alice came into the salon. Audrey was busy sorting out a big box of hairclips, and didn't look up, thinking it was just another customer, something she had got used to during the day. It was only when Alice said,

'Come along, Audrey, it's time for tea,' that the child turned her head.

Sarah noticed at once the set look that crossed Audrey's face. Was there to be another battle? Not if she could help it.

'Come along, Audrey,' she chivvied. 'Do as Alice says. You've been here for hours, you know, and I'll be shutting the shop in a few minutes.'

Audrey got down from her high stool. 'Can I come again?' she asked.

'At the weekend, perhaps, but only if you promise to go to school tomorrow and not make a fuss.'

Audrey's lower lip trembled and tears appeared in her eyes. 'But it isn't my school,' she protested, 'and I won't know anybody.'

'You'll soon make new friends,' Sarah said. 'Just give it a try, will you?'

'All right,' Audrey said with a sigh.

Alice held out her hand to Audrey. 'Mrs Harmon's made some ginger biscuits,' she said. She turned to Sarah. 'I hope it wasn't too awful for you,

Sarah,' she said.

'Not awful at all,' Sarah said with a smile.

Alice visibly shivered. 'Rather you than me, that's all I can say.' She glanced down at Audrey. 'Say thank you to Sarah.'

'Thank you, Sarah,' the child said.

She positively skipped out of the shop, holding on to Alice's hand. Alice looked rather better, Sarah thought. Perhaps she had stayed in bed for most of the day and the rest had done her good.

It was such a lovely evening, the sun beginning to set over the fields in a deep red haze that Sarah decided after her evening meal she would go for a walk. She had been meaning to see where the path running alongside the church led to, but so far she had had scant opportunity to do so.

She put a white cardigan over her shoulders as she thought, despite the sunny day, being still only early June, it could turn chilly later on, and crossed the main road towards the church.

She gave only the briefest glance in the direction of The White House. There was no sign of Gareth's car and the garage door was closed, so he was probably in the house somewhere, but she couldn't see anybody inside the large front sitting room and once she had gone through the gate at the side of the church, knew no-one in The White House would be able to see her anyway, not until she started climbing through the fields, and by then she would probably be too far away to recognise.

There was a scent of newly cut grass in the air and indeed in the garden of one of the bungalows that stood beside the church, an elderly man was walking leisurely up and down with a lawn-mower. He smiled and nodded and Sarah wished him 'Good evening.'

Despite living so near a bus route, this was a very quiet and peaceful area with not much traffic. All Sarah could hear was the lawnmower, a skylark singing overhead and somewhere not too far away, the laughter of children.

Which immediately brought young Audrey to her mind. Had she settled down? Would Gareth have another battle on his hands when he tried to get Audrey to school next morning? After the first few silent minutes in the salon, Audrey had turned out to be chatty and inquisitive, asking questions, walking round the salon, touching, observing but never getting into mischief or doing things she shouldn't.

Sarah had started by saying, 'Let's wash your face, shall we?'

Audrey stared at her. 'I washed it this morning when I got up,' she declared.

'Ah, yes, but you've wept a lot of tears since then, haven't you?' Sarah reminded her.

Audrey merely shrugged her shoulders but submitted to having her face wiped over with a damp flannel and having her hair brushed.

'There!' Sarah said, turning Audrey to look at herself in one of the mirrors. 'Isn't that better?'

Audrey rewarded her with a big grin.

We're going to get on fine, Sarah told herself, and so they had done.

But by now Audrey's bedtime must surely be approaching and what fresh problems would that bring? Sarah remembered her own childhood. How important it was to have a kiss and a hug from her mother before she went to sleep. Audrey must be feeling very bewildered, not understanding why her mother had gone away — how did you explain to a ten-year-old what had happened.

Of course, Gareth, being a doctor, could have told Audrey her mother was in hospital for an operation or because she was sick. But if he had told that white lie, wouldn't it in time pose its own problems when Audrey wondered why her mother didn't come home? Gareth had said Edith was likely to need long term care.

Sarah realised that it couldn't in any way be termed her problem, but it had affected her deeply seeing the child so upset, and she couldn't be there on every occasion, pouring oil on troubled waters.

Wasn't it a fact, she thought, that Alice Bradley was in some ways little more than a child herself? She had certainly displayed some childish attributes during Sarah's own brief acquaintance with her, and she did not really fit Sarah's image of the typical doctor's wife.

But the fact remained Alice was Gareth's wife and Sarah must never lose sight of that fact.

She walked onwards; the field was steep and beyond the narrow track the grass grew knee deep in places. The sun to her right was dipping ever lower. She stopped walking and turned to look backwards, resting her back against a low drystone wall that divided this field and path from a farmer's land where black and white cows were grazing.

Someone was climbing the path she had recently trod, a small figure striding out — a man. He hadn't come much nearer when Sarah realised who it was.

Of course, she could continue on her way, hurrying and hoping he wouldn't catch her up. She could pretend she hadn't noticed him, or she could do the most sensible thing and wait for him to reach her. After all, she couldn't avoid him forever.

His breathlessness told Sarah he had been hurrying. 'A very sensible idea,' he greeted her, 'taking an evening constitutional. I thought I'd join you.'

'Doesn't Alice mind?' Sarah couldn't help saying.

'Why should she? In fact, it was she who spotted you and suggested I go after you. We've got young Audrey safely settled down for the night and Alice is having a bath.' He smiled, the devastating smile that never failed to stir Sarah's emotions. 'So now I have a few minutes to myself.'

Sarah turned away from him and started to walk on. Gareth quickly picked up the pace of her long strides. 'I needed to talk to you, Sarah,' he said.

She didn't look at him, and warded off his remark by saying, 'How is Audrey? No more tantrums, I hope.'

'Not so far, no. She was absolutely fascinated with our bathroom, they don't have one at their flat, so I understand.' He laughed. 'In fact, I thought Mrs Harmon was going to have trouble on her hands when it was time for Audrey to get out the bath.'

'Your housekeeper bathed her?'

Gareth nodded. 'I never even bothered asking Alice to do it. Mrs Harmon doesn't mind. She loves children. Has raised four of her own.'

'Yes, so Alice told me.'

'Anyway, enough talk about Audrey. I'm keeping my fingers crossed about tomorrow morning. I'm living in hope. I want to talk about us.'

Sarah felt herself stiffening. 'There's nothing to talk about,' she said shortly.

'I think there is. I know I set off on the wrong foot and I apologise for that. I should never have tried to kiss you the way I did, but I hope you'll agree we can start again on the right foot.'

Sarah felt anger growing in her. She turned to face him. 'I can't believe I'm hearing this,' she yelled.

Gareth looked perplexed. 'Is there someone else?' he asked.

'Not for me, no, but what about Alice, Gareth? Have you forgotten the little matter of your wife?'

'My wife!' Now it was Gareth's turn to shout. 'Now where on earth did you get the idea that I had . . . ' He broke off, turned half away from her, banging his fists together. 'Alice,' he said.

'You mean she isn't your wife?' Sarah asked, feeling a little stirring of excitement maybe relief inside her.

'Alice is my sister,' Gareth told her.

'But why should she say she's your wife?' But was she really surprised? Wasn't Alice the sort of person who would do and say just what she liked?

Gareth shrugged his shoulders. 'Search me. Probably because at the time she thought it was funny.' He took hold of her hands. 'Believe me, Sarah, I haven't got a wife and I never have had a wife.'

The words sang in Sarah's ears. 'So . . . ' Gareth went on with a tender smile. 'About last night. Was it the silly pass I made at you that offended you, or was it because you thought I was married?'

'Guess!' Sarah said, smiling mischievously.

For an answer, he leaned towards her and this time it wasn't just the brushing of his lips against hers, but a long, lingering kiss. When they broke away, Sarah looked hurriedly around her, but they were completely alone, apart from the grazing cows who hadn't even glanced in their direction.

'I hope you'll allow me to take you out for a meal sometime,' Gareth said softly. 'Of course you'll have to bear in mind that I live a very irregular lifestyle.'

'I know that,' Sarah said.

They were still holding hands, walking along side by side. Sarah was thinking how happy she felt, but a still small voice inside her was whispering, Take it steady, Sarah. You're not ready for a relationship. It's too soon. Too soon.

Then another voice joined in, firmer, stronger. This isn't the same. There can be no comparison. Gareth is kind and gentle. Serious and steady.

And there was something else to be considered. Alice. How would she react if she thought her brother was inviting Sarah out for meals?

'Let me tell Alice I know you're not her husband,' she suggested.

Gareth gave her fingers a squeeze. 'Of course, if that's what you want, but I feel very cross that she could make mischief like that.'

By the time they reached the road, it was dark and the streetlights had come on. The White House curtains had been drawn, and the lights were soft and rosy beyond them.

Sarah felt the peace of the mellow night wash over her and was happy to be going back into her little flat to draw her own curtains and sit in the lamp light, thinking about Gareth.

Then she saw the last car in the line, impatiently honking at the trolley bus moving slowly in front of it. A dark car, smooth and sleek; a man at the wheel, looking tense, leaning forward, glowering out of the windscreen.

He didn't look to the right or left. He probably never even noticed the couple waiting to cross the road, but Sarah knew who it was. She recognised the car, she recognised the impatience of the driver.

She felt her fingers clasping Gareth's tightly. He laughed softly in the darkness.

'Steady on, you're breaking my fingers,' he said.

She relaxed her hold. 'Sorry!'

Her heart was starting to thump. He had found her. Oh, perhaps he wasn't sure just where she lived, but it was him and he was looking for her. There could be no other reason for his being in the area. He called the outlying villages of Heaton 'backwaters'. He preferred buildings and noise and bright lights. He wouldn't be seen dead here unless he had a good reason for coming.

She was that reason, but she couldn't say anything to Gareth. He had enough on his plate without her troubles and besides, how could she tell him what a fool she had been to get herself mixed up with someone like Tim Mercer in the first place?

4

Sarah slept badly that night and it wasn't because Gareth was in her thoughts. Despite her original excitement at the prospect of going out with Gareth, the fear of seeing Tim Mercer had overshadowed that.

She ought to have known he wouldn't let it go. He had once told her that she was his and nobody else would ever have her. It was his possessiveness and domination that had made her finally break free of him. It wouldn't have been enough simply to tell Tim it was over; she had to get right away from him and she acted swiftly and secretly, finding out about the salon in Fenton which, thankfully had accommodation too, fixing it all up and moving in when Tim was in London.

Perhaps, she reflected, as she tossed and turned in bed, she hadn't gone far enough. Perhaps she should have left Heaton far behind, moved to another part of the country, but she couldn't bring herself to do that.

But now, Tim had found her. Or at least was on to her. It was only a matter of time.

The following day, Sarah went through the motions, chatting to her customers, dispensing cups of tea. She saw nothing of Gareth, or Alice, and it seemed there had been no repeat performance at The White House. Just after half past three, Audrey burst into the salon.

Sarah was sweeping up the cuttings from her last customer and it would be ten minutes before the next arrived. She smiled at the effervescent Audrey.

'Been to school, have you?' she asked.

'I've just got back,' Audrey said, eyeing the plate of digestive biscuits hopefully.

'So I expect you'll be having your tea in a few minutes.'

'Well . . . yes . . . ' Audrey agreed,

'but it's ages since I had my dinner.' She pulled a face. 'It was horrible. Cabbage. I hate cabbage. And rice pudding.'

She shuddered and her eyes strayed back to the plate of biscuits.

Laughing Sarah picked it up and held it out. 'Just one,' she warned.

Audrey didn't need a second invitation. Seeing the child had brightened Sarah up considerably. Taken her mind off her problems, if only temporarily. Audrey looked bright and happy. Her hair ribbon had inevitably come undone and she had one white sock up and one down, but it was hard to imagine how she had been the previous day.

'What was it like, being at school?' Sarah asked, as Audrey sat in one of the hairdressing chairs, swinging backwards and forwards, munching her biscuit.

'All right. Better than my other school.'

'And have you found a friend yet?'

Audrey stared at her. 'Lots of friends.

I'm going to ask Gareth if I can ask Mary Dawson to tea on Sunday.'

Oh dear, Sarah thought, what would Alice have to say about that?

'Does Alice know you're here, Audrey?' she asked, realising that the child had probably run straight round here after being dropped off. Gareth had told her the day before that, because he wouldn't always be available to collect Audrey from school, one of the teachers who lived in the area was going to bring her home.

Sarah could tell by the way Audrey's eyes slid away from her that she had been right in her assumption.

'Alice doesn't like me,' Audrey mumbled.

'Of course she does,' Sarah cried. 'You mustn't say things like that,' but the child was probably right and Alice would have no hesitation in making her feelings known.

'She's mean. She says mean things and she . . . '

'She what?' Sarah prompted.

Audrey went on in a rush. 'She hurts me. She takes hold of my arm and she squeezes. And she's got funny eyes.'

Sarah felt a flutter of disturbance. 'Have you told Gareth?' she asked.

Audrey shook her head. 'No. I don't want to.' She looked into Sarah's eyes. 'Tell tale tit, your tongue will split,' she quoted.

Sarah went and put her arm around Audrey's shoulders. 'Well, you must be a good girl for Alice, Audrey, don't upset her.'

She felt that was avoiding the issue and went on, wishing to justify her words. 'She's not very well, you know. She had a bad sickness when she was a young girl, and she needs to rest a lot and be quiet.'

'All right,' Audrey nodded solemnly, 'I'll try.'

She finished off her biscuit and turned to leave the salon. Sarah watched her. Just at that moment she seemed a forlorn little figure and Sarah sincerely hoped that there wasn't any real problem with Alice because if there was she would certainly consider it her duty to interfere and tell Gareth.

She got through the rest of the day and went up to her flat which suddenly seemed quiet and empty. She didn't have much appetite so made herself cheese on toast, eating it curled up on the sofa listening to the radio. She wondered briefly when she would see Gareth again. She knew he was extremely busy, but she hoped he would contact her soon so they could arrange a date.

She had finished the washing up and thought she might wash her hair when there was a knock at the street door.

Gareth, she thought, but in the next moment it occurred to her that it might be Tim and she stopped in her tracks. The knocking came again, even louder. Whoever it was sounded very impatient. It must be Tim! He had found her and she knew from past experience that he wouldn't give up.

She crossed the narrow passage from

the sitting-room to her bedroom that overlooked the front of the salon, peeping out from behind the curtain, looking from left to right. If it was Tim, his Jaguar would be somewhere near.

He wasn't known for walking even a hundred yards if he didn't need to, but she could see no car in the street at all, except for one across the road that was usually there.

She stood on her tiptoes and tried to look out of the slightly-open top window to see who was at the door.

Alice! She might have known. What did she want? She was banging on the door with both fists by now. Sarah had no choice but to go and let her in.

'About time,' Alice remarked walking straight past Sarah and up the stairs. Today she seemed to be able to climb the steep flight with amazing speed and she was already sitting down when Sarah went into the sitting-room.

'What has Audrey been saying about me?' was her opening remark.

'Only that she thinks you don't like

her.' Sarah decided that honesty was the best policy.

'And now the cheeky little minx thinks she's got you on her side. 'I'll tell Sarah if you hurt me again,' she taunted me.'

'So you admit you did hurt her then?' Sarah sat down.

Alice's pale eyes narrowed. 'Of course I didn't. I might have grabbed hold of her arm, but she drove me to it. She goes in my room, fiddling with my things. I caught her using my Californian Poppy perfume spray.'

Sarah suppressed a smile. Isn't that what all little girls did, sneak into their big sister's room? And wasn't Alice just like a big sister, at least in Audrey's mind?

'I'm glad you find it amusing,' Alice snapped.

'She means no harm, Alice,' Sarah said. 'She's probably never been in a house like yours.'

'I'm quite sure she hasn't, but she's got a perfectly good bedroom of her own. She's got some of her own toys. Gareth brought them back with him, and Mrs Harmon, silly woman, has brought her some cuddly toys that belong to her grandchild.'

'But I bet she's lonely,' Sarah remarked. 'It's all been such a big change for her and she seems to be settling down at school all right, doesn't she?'

Alice got up and flounced across the room. Who is the child here, Sarah couldn't help wondering. 'I am simply dreading the summer holidays,' Alice said. 'Last year Gareth took me away for a couple of weeks, to the seaside. We rented a bungalow. It was wonderful. No phone calls in the middle of the night. No call-outs. Just Gareth and me.'

'A husband and wife together, eh?' Sarah couldn't help saying.

Sarah was glad that Alice had the grace to blush. 'He's told you then?'

'Of course he has.'

'So you didn't believe me when I said

Gareth was my husband?' Alice asked.

'Of course I did. I'm not a mind reader.'

'So how come he told you then? In what context did it come up in the conversation?'

'Oh, for goodness sake,' Sarah cried, determined that she wasn't going to tell Alice anything about the attempted kiss and her reaction to it.

'It doesn't matter, anyway,' Alice said airily, coming to sit on the sofa again, leaning back as though she had come to stay for the evening. 'Gareth and I belong together. He's ten years older than I am, you know. He's looked after me since our father was killed in the war.

'We lost our mother when I was two and Gareth has always been there for me. When I got rheumatic fever and it was touch and go for a while, Gareth promised me he would never leave me. He's thirty-four now, nearly thirty-five and he's never had a serious girlfriend.' She got up and smiled sweetly at Sarah.

'I just thought you ought to know,' she concluded and walked slowly out of the room without a backward glance.

Sarah spoke out loud. 'So that's telling me,' she said.

And suddenly she found the whole conversation amusing and started to laugh, but her laughter didn't last long, because she knew what she was up against now. It was very early days, she still had Tim Mercer to deal with, but Sarah instinctively knew that Gareth Bradley would not be the sort of man to indulge in a light flirtation.

The next morning there was a note through her letter box. Gone to a medical council meeting today, but I'll be through by early afternoon. How about that date? Shall I pick you up at seven? LOVE, Gareth.

He'd written the word love in capital letters which probably meant nothing, but still made Sarah feel excited. She wondered where Gareth planned taking her. There were a few good restaurants in Heaton. She'd been to one or two with Tim in the past. The only worry was, what would she do if Tim happened to be in the one they went to?

She decided to go along with whatever he had arranged. She was determined to enjoy herself and she spent a great deal of time getting ready. Having a long, hot soak in the bath, dressing with care and putting on some light touches of make up.

She surveyed herself in the full length mirror in her bedroom. She was tall, slim with short blonde well-cut hair. Her former mentor and employer, Robert Cardine, still did her hair for her. In fact she should really make another appointment with him before long, she supposed.

Sarah had chosen a black pencil-slim skirt with a kick pleat and a silky white blouse on which she'd turned up the collar. She'd put on black court shoes and a pair of long silver earrings that had been her mother's. She wouldn't need a jacket as the evenings were warm.

She was ready just on time and the knock on the street door told her Gareth, too, was a good timekeeper.

When he saw her he whistled. 'You look stunning,' he said.

Sarah smiled shyly. Gareth took her breath away. He wore a casual jacket and dark trousers over a white shirt. His car was waiting by the kerb.

'Where are we going?' Sarah asked as Gareth opened the car door for her.

'Well, I hope I'm taking you somewhere you've never been before,' he said. 'We'll go through Thorley and take the main road out to Dunfirth. There's a lovely restaurant there, newly opened, but highly recommended to me. It's called Fernlea and I've reserved us a table. How does that sound?'

'It sounds wonderful!' Sarah cried, so relieved that they weren't going to go anywhere near Heaton.

Now she could really look forward to the evening. As they pulled away from the kerb, Gareth glanced at her. 'I'll ask just one thing of you, Sarah,' he began, 'no questions about Alice and Audrey. They are strictly taboo tonight. Agreed?'

Sarah nodded. 'Agreed.'

The evening was everything Sarah could have hoped. The food and wine were excellent, the restaurant certainly living up to its reputation. Courteous, attentive staff, soft lights, unobtrusive music. And Gareth. Charming, attentive, funny. So very different from Tim who had always been over-brash, trying to impress, flashing his wallet about and often, making quite unnecessary compliments.

It had often amazed Sarah why on earth she had tolerated him for as long as she had. But now was not a time to even give Tim Mercer a second thought.

It was dark when they finally left the restaurant and the roads were quiet. Gareth drove carefully and Sarah, feeling a little sleepy, perhaps from the wine, rested her head on the headrest and closed her eyes. She had this wonderful feeling of being able to put all her trust into Gareth. Not only because of his careful driving but because of the type of man he was.

She could never imagine him jumping up and overturning a coffee table because Sarah had dared to disagree with him, as Tim had done in the past. Or slamming the phone down on her when she had a heavy cold and had said she didn't feel up to going out.

Gareth was the sort of man who would always be there for a person, whether a friend, a patient, or in Alice's case, a sister. This knowledge made Sarah feel good.

Gareth pulled up outside the salon. 'From your door to your door,' he announced.

Sarah stirred, stifling a yawn. Gareth's eyebrows rose. 'Boring you, am I?' he asked.

'Oh, no, I'm sorry, I'm just so sleepy.' Sarah apologised. 'I've had such a wonderful evening. Thank you for asking me.'

'The first of many evenings out, I

hope,' Gareth said with a warm smile, 'my job and family commitments notwithstanding.'

'I hope so too,' Sarah breathed.

Gareth leant forward and kissed her. Then, after they had got out of the car, he kissed her again, putting his arms around her. They stood under the streetlight, holding one another close.

'You're so beautiful, Sarah,' Gareth told her.

'Thank you.'

'But I must let you go. Another day tomorrow.'

'Do you like being a doctor?' she asked him.

Gareth seemed to consider the question carefully. Then he said, 'Yes, I do. I wanted to be a doctor ever since I was a boy. And when the National Health Service was introduced in 1948, I committed myself to that.'

Reluctantly they said goodnight, kissing for the last time and Gareth waited outside the street until he saw Sarah's lights go on upstairs. Then he got back in his car and drove round to The White House.

What neither of them had noticed was the sleek dark red car parked farther up the road. Nor the expression on the driver's face as with barely concealed anger he started up the engine and swerved out into the main road, heading down the hill to Heaton.

5

The next few days were quiet and uneventful. Audrey continued to visit the salon whenever she got the opportunity. Sarah even let her go up to the flat, but she saw nothing of Alice and precious little of Gareth. Alice, Sarah thought ruefully, she could do well without, but Gareth . . .

She missed him. She thought about him constantly and couldn't wait for another chance to go out with him; another opportunity to be held by him, and kissed by him, but she had to content herself with seeing him smile and wave as he walked out to his car; a couple of times she was looking out the window when he walked down the garden.

Unlike Alice, Gareth stopped to admire the flowers, to pick a weed here and there. On Sunday morning, he even took the time and trouble to do the grass cutting, walking backwards and forwards, in his shirt sleeves. When he looked up and saw her, and his face lit up in one of his lovely smiles, Sarah was made up for the day.

But it seemed Gareth was busy and who was she to interfere with a dedicated general practitioner who not only had patients to care for, but a semi-invalid sister and a demanding small child.

On Saturdays, Sarah closed the salon at noon. She generally had a light lunch and either went for a walk, or did some shopping in Thorley, walking down the hill and taking the trolley bus back. Surprisingly, Thorley had several small shops and Sarah found she could usually get what she needed without having to face the trip into Heaton itself. Though she knew she couldn't put off that journey for ever.

There was her mother to visit, for one thing, who lived in an old people's home on the far side of Heaton. Mrs

Mallinson was over seventy, Sarah being the only child of her old age and was now getting a bit senile. She had lived in the home for just over a year.

Usually, Sarah was a regular visitor, but what with the move and her fear of bumping into Tim, she had neglected her duty and this state of affairs couldn't be allowed to continue for much longer.

She made up her mind that some time that Saturday she would make the effort. Who knew, it may be one of her mother's better days, when she was lucid and responsive and Sarah would be able to tell her all about Gareth.

She had noticed that the sky had clouded over a little and was contemplating whether she should take her umbrella, when there came a knock on the outside door. It seemed ages since this had happened. Perhaps it was Gareth. Oh, she hoped so, she certainly didn't want it to be Alice, bringing one of her bad moods, or her over-excited friendliness with her.

'Hello, Sarah,' Tim said smoothly as she opened the door.

If it hadn't been that he had already put his foot in the doorway Sarah knew she would have slammed the door in his face.

'What do you want?' she asked, trying to keep her voice steady.

'To see you, of course. Aren't you going to invite me in?'

He'd placed his hand on either side of the doorframe. She knew he wouldn't go away so she had no choice but to let him come in. The lobby downstairs was small and they were standing very close together. Sarah could smell his aftershave lotion, a tangy, sharp perfume, so well remembered.

He followed her upstairs and she was aware that he would be looking her up and down. Once in the flat she moved as far away from him as she could.

'How did you find me?' she demanded.

He was wearing, as always, an immaculate suit, a perfectly knotted tie.

Robert Cardine was his hair stylist too and he had obviously only recently had it cut. His narrow face was suave and his slate grey eyes all-seeing.

'Nice place,' he remarked, ignoring her question, turning his head this way and that to look disparagingly around the room.

He didn't mean it. He owned an impressive Victorian terrace house on the very edge of Heaton. He also owned his own antiques business and enjoyed holidaying in Spain. Sarah had always been able to manage wriggling out of accompanying him on one of his trips, much to his annoyance.

'You haven't answered my question,' she said coldly.

Without invitation, Tim sat down, hitching up his dark trousers with their knife-edge creases.

'How do you think I knew where to find you?' he threw at her. 'Your mother, of course.'

Sarah sat down. 'My mother?' He had been to see her mother?

Again without invitation, or permission, Tim took out a silver cigarette case and matching lighter, old and valuable of course, and calmly lit a cigarette blowing perfect smoke rings into the air.

'What's wrong with that? I've been before with you, haven't I?'

Tim went on, 'The matron let me in without a murmur.' (She would, of course, Tim could charm the birds off a tree when he wanted to; hadn't she leaned that fact to her cost?) 'Oh, she's very efficient at her job, mind you, she stood there like Cerberus guarding the gates of Hades, but when she realised who I was, she let me in. And your mother was delightful.

'It took a couple of visits before I got any sense out of the old girl and then she handed me this scrap of paper. The only thing was, it had been torn, your mother said she'd spilt her tea over it, and there was only part of an address. 'Off Fenton Road South' it said. Your handwriting though, Sarah, quite unmistakable. So I set out to find you. The first time I drove right past here, it was getting dark and I'd had a few drinks.'

The night she'd been walking with Gareth, Sarah remembered.

'Then I came here during the day and I saw the salon on the corner and put two and two together. I could see you in there, Sarah, snipping away. I also saw a postman delivering some letters to the side door and, well, looking up, it didn't take Sherlock Holmes to deduce you were living over the shop, as it were.'

Tim was a master of sarcasm, one of his many attributes.

She said nothing and Tim looked around him. 'No ash tray?' he queried, shaking his partly smoked cigarette and causing grey ash to drift on to the carpet. She noticed not a flake of it hit his immaculate trousers.

She got up quickly and handed him a small white dish from the shelf which he set with great care on the sofa arm.

'The next time I saw you,' he went on, staring at her intently so that she had to look away and a feeling of dread came over her because she had seen that look on Tim's face before. He knew something about her and Gareth! What and how she couldn't guess, but his next words left her in no doubt, 'was a few nights ago. When I got here, fully intending to knock on your door, the whole place was in darkness. In fact, the whole dreary street was completely dead.

'Then, a car came round the corner and two people got out. A man and a woman. They stood under a street light and feeble though that light was, I could see them plainly and one of them was you, Sarah. The other was a tall, quite good looking man who seemed most intent on holding you and kissing you.'

Sarah jumped up, 'Stop it, stop it!' she yelled, feeling tears of frustration and anger alarmingly close. She mustn't cry, she wouldn't cry.

Tim's fixed smile vanished like magic. 'Didn't waste much time, did you, Sarah, in finding another beau.'

'Dr Bradley is a friend,' she cried.

Tim's eyebrows rose. 'Oh, a doctor, eh? Another professional man. Well, I'll give it to you, Sarah, you know how to pick them.'

'What I do is no business of yours, Tim.'

Tim shot to his feet and with two strides was in front of her by the window, holding her arms tightly. 'That's where you're wrong. It's very much to do with me. We were going to get married, remember.'

'No, we weren't. I never said I would marry you.'

'You know me, Sarah, I'm very persuasive.'

Sarah tried desperately to break free of him, but he was much taller, much stronger than she was.

'I would never have married you, Tim Mercer and I want you to leave now, please,' Sarah cried. 'I moved house and got a new job to escape you. Apparently I didn't go far enough.'

'Nowhere is far enough, my dear Sarah,' Tim said menacingly.

He tried to pull her closer and as Sarah struggled, he head turned to the window and she saw Gareth in the garden. He had come out of the open french windows and Audrey ran past him to the other end of the garden. Gareth threw the ball he was carrying and Audrey caught it, laughing, and threw it back, but not very expertly and Gareth missed it and bent to pick it up. When he did so he looked up and saw them standing by the window.

Sarah wished she could call out, 'Gareth, Gareth, help me please,' but all she could think of was getting Tim away from the window, so that Gareth would not see them together and possibly misconstrue the situation, but it was too late. Tim had looked out of the window as well. His hold on Sarah slackened, but she still could not get away from him.

'Ah, the good doctor,' he drawled, and as Gareth continued to glance upwards, whilst Audrey jumped up and down impatiently waiting for him to throw the ball again, Tim caught her tightly and kissed her with great ferocity, bruising her lips, stifling her.

When he released her and Sarah looked down, Gareth had disappeared and a disappointed Audrey was yelling out and running back into the house after him.

At last Tim left, leaving Sarah scared and tense and not knowing which way to turn. He had promised he would be back and Sarah had no reason to doubt his word. Now he knew where she lived he would never be off her doorstep, and the knowledge was frightening.

But more worrying was what Gareth must be thinking. He wouldn't have been able to assess the situation — how could he? — and would assume that Sarah had been kissing Tim of her own free will. Should she go round there and explain what had happened? But if she did, she would have to go into the whole matter of Tim in her life, and that in itself was yet another worry.

For now, she decided to let the matter go. She would go and visit her mother, being with the old lady would surely take her mind off her troubles. Later, when she felt calmer she would go round to The White House and hope Gareth would be there and would be willing to talk to her.

But later that afternoon, feeling more than a little drained after spending a couple of hours in her mother's company on what had turned out to be an especially bad day for Mrs Mallinson, Sarah stepped off the trolley bus by the church and, as she started to cross the road, she saw Gareth in the front garden.

Her heart lurched at the sight of him. He wasn't doing anything in particular, he just seemed to be admiring the display of flowers in the neat, colourful borders, his hand in his pockets, his head bent. But he was alone and Sarah knew she couldn't let this opportunity go.

She stood at the end of the drive. 'Hello, Gareth,' she said softly.

He twisted round. For a split second he looked pleased to see her, then he frowned and Sarah's worst fears were realised.

'Sarah,' he said curtly.

Sarah took the plunge, 'Gareth . . . about what you saw earlier . . . ' but Gareth broke in, holding up his hand.

'I don't wish to know, Sarah. It's none of my business.'

'It wasn't what it seemed. I did have a relationship with Tim, but it was over before I moved here.' But that wasn't strictly true, she had merely run away from the life she had with Tim, she had never actually broken off with him. 'He found out where I lived and turned up unexpectedly. He saw you in the garden, Gareth, and that's why he kissed me. I . . . I didn't want him to.'

Her words sounded feeble to her own ears and Gareth seemed completely unmoved by them.

'I've said I don't want to know,' he told her. 'But if what you say is true, why didn't you tell me about this Tim? You knew how I felt about you.'

Should she be encouraged by this admission or only more dismayed at what she might have lost?

'I . . . I don't know,' was all she could say.

She heard footsteps on the gravel drive and saw Alice coming round from the back of the house. Facing Alice was the last thing Sarah wanted.

'Sarah!' Alice cried. 'Where have you been hiding yourself? Are you coming in for tea?'

'Sorry, Alice, I can't. Not now.' She turned and started walking quickly to the corner, disappearing round it and out of their sight.

Sarah kept to herself for the rest of the day. Early in the evening someone came to the door. Taking no chances, she went into the bedroom and looked out of the window. It was Audrey.

Feeling awful, Sarah moved away and ignored Audrey's repeated banging on the door.

She didn't want to be with anyone at all. But Monday morning she had to open up the salon as usual, she couldn't let down her regular customers and in a way, chatting to them, keeping busy did help her.

She generally closed the salon for an hour at twelve noon and went up to the flat for some lunch, but when she got there she remembered she had used the last milk at breakfast, so picking up her purse she ran down the stairs again and across the road to the small general store next to the pub. When she came out she saw Tim's unmistakable Jaguar parked outside The White House and her heart sank.

What was he doing there? As she watched, she saw him climb out of the car and start walking up the drive. Oh dear, what was he up to? However, before Tim reached the front door, because it was obvious that's where he was heading, Gareth came out on to the broad front step and Sarah saw Tim's bright, friendly smile. He held out his hand but Gareth only glared at him.

Sarah knew it would be best if she returned unobserved to her flat, but she couldn't, because she knew Tim was capable of saying anything he chose to Gareth about her, whether or not it was true, so she crossed the road and approached The White House.

She could hear Tim talking, shrugging his shoulders, an expression of innocence on his face. Gareth, on the other hand, was beginning to look increasingly angry and Sarah noticed that his fists were clenched.

She heard Tim saying, 'I'm sorry, old boy, but I thought you ought to know how things are.'

Gareth spoke at last. 'I don't believe you. Sarah would have told me if she was engaged to be married.'

'Getting a little nervous I expect,' Tim went on smoothly, 'with the wedding day approaching.'

Sarah called out from the gateway, clutching the bottle of milk in her hand. 'Don't listen to him, Gareth, it's all lies . . . '

Both men looked up and saw her and Tim's smile became even more pronounced, but Sarah did not miss the steely glint in his grey eyes.

'I was just explaining to Dr Bradley about you and me, Sarah,' Tim announced and he held out his hand to her, as though, Sarah thought, she would run to him and take hold of it.

'There is no you and me,' Sarah cried, 'how many times do I have to tell you?'

Gareth spoke with careful restraint. 'Why don't you just go away and leave Sarah alone?'

Tim turned back to face him. 'I can't do that.' He said.

'Well, please yourself, but I'm far too busy to stand on the doorstep listening to you,' and Gareth turned to go back through the front door.

But Tim was too quick for him. He

lurched forward and grabbed Gareth by the shoulder. 'Just one minute . . . ' he yelled and now the smooth smile had disappeared and the real Tim was very much in evidence. 'Don't turn your back on me you . . . '

Gareth placed his hands in the middle of Tim's chest and gave a hefty shove. Tim tottered backwards and sprawled on to the gravel. Whereupon Gareth grabbed him by the lapels of his smart jacket and hauled him upwards, pulling him very close.

'Don't make me do something I'll regret,' he warned in a deadly voice. 'Just get back in your smart car and drive away. All right?' and with a little flick of his wrists he released Tim before dusting himself down.

Tim was livid, but Sarah could tell he was also scared. He was a typical bully; he liked to domineer women but he had probably never been manhandled before and he didn't like that.

Without a word of retaliation he marched down the drive, totally ignoring Sarah and got in his car, starting it up and doing a three-point turn into the main road, then driving off at speed back down the hill towards Heaton.

Sarah was shaking and Gareth must have noticed because he walked down the drive towards her. 'I'm sorry, Sarah,' he said in a voice that wasn't unkind, 'that was a dreadful scene. As a doctor I should know better than to brawl on my own doorstep but there was something about that fellow that made me see red.'

'Can you also now see what I'm up against?' Sarah asked. 'He won't leave me alone and I don't know what to do.'

But Gareth made no move to comfort her. Rather did he seem awkward, on edge, as though he wanted to get away from her.

'Sarah . . . ' he began cautiously, but said no more as the telephone shrilled through the open front door.

Gareth turned and went inside to answer it. Sarah could hear him talking sharply and after a few seconds she turned and started walking back to the flat, but before she had a chance to put the key in the door, she heard running footsteps and Gareth appeared round the corner. One glance at his face told her that something was wrong.

'What's the matter?' she asked.

'It's Audrey. She's gone missing. That was the headmaster on the phone. Audrey went to school this morning, but at last break she couldn't be found. She went to the cloakroom with the other children to wash her hands, then she simply disappeared. I'm going down to the school now. Will you come with me, please? I . . . can't let Alice know, not yet.'

His eyes were beseeching her. 'Of course I'll come,' Sarah told him and deposited her bottle of milk on the doorstep.

Lunch and the salon would have to wait.

6

Jeffrey Wallace, the headmaster of Thorley Infants and Junior school, was a tall, well-built man, around fifty, Sarah guessed, with thick, greying hair and kind eyes. She imagined he was a good headmaster, firm but fair and he was obviously very concerned about Audrey's absence.

Sarah and Gareth sat by Mr Wallace's desk, whilst he went over the details of what he knew, twirling a pencil in his fingers which seemed to indicate his agitation.

'Audrey was definitely here till lunch break,' he said. 'I spoke to her myself.' He gave a little smile. 'Actually she was running along a corridor, nearly barged into me. I tut-tutted and waggled my finger at her and she went away more slowly.'

'How did she seem?' Gareth asked.

'Well, to be honest, she has seemed a little distracted. After the initial problems with her, which only lasted two or three days, she appeared to be fine. She's made friends, she's good at sports and her arithmetic and reading skills are, I would say, above average for her age.'

'In what way distracted?' Gareth questioned.

Sarah could feel the tension in him. He was Audrey's guardian and he must be really worried about her where-abouts.

'On edge. Particularly this morning. Restless. I'm telling you what her form teacher, Miss Etchells, told me, of course, the fleeting glimpse I had of her personally was too quick for me to pick up any danger signals. And, another thing, Miss Etchells said she saw evidence of tears on Audrey's face.'

'Didn't this Miss Etchells bother to ask Audrey what was wrong?' Gareth's voice was sharp.

'Yes, she told me she did,' Mr Wallace

said, pacifying, 'but Audrey said there was nothing wrong.'

'And then she suddenly vanished into thin air?' Gareth went on.

Mr Wallace put down his pencil. 'It would seem so. No-one can actually remember her movements. You know what it's like at break time, I'm sure.' He gave another of his kind smiles. 'Pandemonium. It was only when the teacher on lunch duty noticed her chair at the table was empty, and she couldn't be found in the cloakroom, that the alarm was raised. I telephoned you right away, Dr Bradley.'

He turned to look at Sarah who so far had said nothing. Now she asked a question of her own; something that had been bothering her ever since she heard about Audrey's disappearance.

'Was Audrey being bullied do you think?'

She could tell by Gareth's expression that he had wondered the same thing, but Mr Wallace looked astounded.

'Bullied?' he cried, sitting bolt upright

in his chair. 'I'm quite sure she wasn't. Bullying has never been a problem at this school.'

Gareth gave a thin smile. 'There's always a first time for everything, headmaster,' he said.

'All the same, I would stake my reputation that no-one was bullying the child. She had made friends easily, she was well-liked, popular.'

'So why is she missing? We can only assume she left the school of her own accord and something must have caused her to do that.'

Sarah was beginning to get a distinctly uneasy feeling. She remembered when Audrey last came to the salon. How she hadn't wanted to go home because of Alice.

'Alice is mean to me,' she had said. 'She hurts me.'

Sarah had made light of it, but could that be the reason? Was Audrey indeed being bullied, but by Alice not another child at school?

No, no, it couldn't be true. Alice was

strange, childish in many ways, but deliberately cruel? She couldn't be.

But the thought would not go away and Sarah knew she had no choice but to tell Gareth of her fears. Before they left the school, it had been decided that, should Audrey not come back within the next hour or so the police would have to be called in. Sarah knew Gareth did not want it to come to that and as they sat in his car outside the playground he turned to Sarah.

'Rack your brains, Sarah,' he said. 'Where do you think Audrey can have gone? She doesn't know the area well. I've taken her for walks up the fields a few times. Do you think she can have gone up there?'

'Perhaps,' Sarah said. 'But that would mean her coming all up the hill from Thorley. I think it's more likely that she will have run into the field behind the school, the one where they play and then gone farther. If she was very upset she might have simply run blind and have got lost.'

Gareth turned off the ignition. 'Then let's not waste any more time. We'll look in the most obvious place first.'

'Won't Alice be worried where you are?' Sarah asked.

'I doubt it. She had gone to lie down before I came to the door and . . . dealt with that fellow. She's probably taken one of her pills and not even Mrs Harmon's hoovering will disturb her. I've got to get back for late afternoon surgery, of course, but,' he glanced at his watch, 'we've plenty of time before that.' He opened the car door, then hesitated. 'How about you? Will you have customers waiting?'

Probably, she thought, but that was too bad. This was an emergency. She shook her head. 'No appointments till three,' she lied.

Gareth smiled and touched her hand. 'Thank you, Sarah,' he said, 'for being here.'

How long would things stay like this, Sarah wondered? Once Audrey was found, would Gareth remember, not that she was a good friend who was there to give him encouragement and support, but that she had not been honest with him; that she had unwittingly been the cause of his losing control when he pushed Tim?

She dismissed these thoughts and they got out of the car. As they went round the back of the school towards the fields, Sarah remembered what she had to tell Gareth.

'Audrey told me something rather worrying the other day,' she remarked.

'What was what?' Gareth said, looking sharply at her.

'She said Alice had been mean to her. Pinching her.'

Gareth actually laughed. 'Oh, what nonsense!' he cried.

'I don't think it is,' Sarah said, 'and in the light of what's happened . . . ' her voice trailed off.

'So you're suggesting that Audrey has run away because of something Alice did to her?'

'Well Audrey was quite serious when

she told me and I believe her.'

'Oh, come, I know Alice is no angel, but to deliberately harm a child . . . '

'She has mood swings, Gareth. I haven't known her long, but I've noticed that. She may not have really hurt Audrey but I believe she's certainly tried to scare her.'

Sarah could tell that Gareth was far from convinced and now that she had spoken of her fears she did begin to have serious doubts that she might have made the accusation prematurely. It was just that she was trying to find a reason why Audrey had gone missing.

Gareth walked on, not looking at her. Then he said, 'Well, we'd better wait and see what Alice has to say before we accuse her out of hand. And Audrey as well, of course. I'm sure we'll find her before long.'

Sarah hoped he was right, but the search of the fields near the school brought them no joy. Reluctantly they went back to the car, both of them looking out for any sign of the child all the way back to Fenton.

'I'm going up the fields behind the church,' Gareth announced, drawing up outside the salon.

Sarah could see two women waiting outside and felt a pang of guilt. 'I've got to go to the salon, Gareth,' she said.

'That's all right. I understand. Thanks for your help so far.'

But had she been any help really? Had she upset Gareth once again by accusing his sister like she had? She could feel they were drawing further and further away from one another.

As soon as she was able to close the salon she went straight round to The White House, hoping against hope that Audrey had turned up, but when Gareth opened the door, she could tell by looking at his face that she hadn't.

'Come in,' he invited.

'No news?'

Gareth shook his head. 'I'm going to phone the police. I can't put it off any longer.'

Alice was in the sitting-room, her legs

curled under her on the sofa. She was dabbing at her eyes with a handkerchief and Sarah could see that she had been crying.

'Oh, Alice!' Sarah cried in a spontaneous show of sympathy.

She moved towards the sofa, but Alice sat up sharply and her blue eyes flashed annoyance.

'So you think I've driven Audrey away, do you?' she accused. 'Gareth has told me what you said. How dare you suggest I might hurt her!'

'I was only saying what Audrey told me,' Sarah said in her own defence.

'You accused me once before and I told you then I hadn't touched her.' She dabbed at her eyes again. 'I thought we were friends.'

Sarah couldn't bring herself to say, 'Yes, we are,' because, after all, it came down to one of them lying, Alice or Audrey and Sarah did not miss how Alice's eyes had slid away from her. She had seen that look before, notably when Alice had said Gareth was her husband.

She knew she was right.

Gareth came into the room. 'The police are on their way,' he said.

Alice began to sob. Gareth went to comfort her. 'Don't, Alice,' he begged, 'we'll find her, safe and sound, promise you.' He gave Sarah a brief, stern look. 'See how upset she is, and your accusations haven't helped matters, Sarah.'

She felt she was in the way. She could do nothing more at this stage. She stood up. 'I'll go home,' she said, 'when the police know anything, please let me know.'

'Of course I will,' Gareth told her and turned back to his seemingly heart-broken sister.

Sarah spent a miserable early evening; she hadn't eaten since breakfast and she forced herself to swallow some soup and nibble at a slice of toast, but she had no appetite for food.

Had the police been next door yet? What were they planning to do? She felt so helpless not knowing just what was going on but she couldn't simply go round there. She couldn't face either Gareth's condemnation or Alice's crocodile tears.

At nine o'clock Sarah decided she had had enough. She was going to go out for a walk. It wasn't dark yet and she had to clear her head, but as she opened the street door she almost collided with Gareth who was just about to knock on it.

Immediately she knew that Audrey had been found. 'We've got her home, Sarah,' Gareth said, the relief so obvious on his face.

'Oh, Gareth!' Sarah cried and without thinking she leaned forward and kissed his cheek. 'Is she all right?'

'She's fine. I've fetched Mrs Harmon round — you knew she didn't live in, didn't you — and she's given Audrey a bath and is staying with her till I get back.' He paused then went on, 'Were you going out?'

'Only for a walk. Where was Audrey? Has she told you anything yet?'

'She's told me enough.' Gareth's voice was suddenly grim. 'Sarah, I need to talk to you. May I come in?'

'Of course.'

They went back up the stairs. Once in the flat, Sarah said, 'Would you like some tea?'

'Not just now, thank you.' He gave a weak smile. 'Later, perhaps. Sit down, Sarah.'

She did so, wondering what Gareth was about to tell her.

'You were right,' he said, 'about Alice. Oh, God, I can't believe it, but I've seen the bruises. On the tops of Audrey's arms; on her back. The child was terrified. But that isn't why Audrey ran away, she had put up with the abuse ever since she arrived. No, it was because Alice had started saying things about her mother, that's what triggered off the running away.'

'What sort of things?' Sarah asked, though she could well imagine.

'Saying Edith was mad, that she'd been locked up and wouldn't ever be coming out.' He paused and ran his hand through his hair. 'The poor child went on and on once she'd started. The whispering campaign began at the weekend and on Monday morning Audrey decided to try to find her mother.

'She went down to the main road that runs on the other side of Thorley and set off walking. She knew, because she'd been there with me, that buses ran along that road towards Heaton, just as they do down Fenton road outside here, and she thought she could walk into Heaton and get to the train station and eventually, poor little love, to where her mother was.' He gave a little smile. 'She had no money of course.'

'But where did the police actually find her?' Sarah asked.

'In a bus shelter. It's five miles to Heaton from Thorley and Audrey did remarkably well by covering almost the whole distance, but she got tired and she went into the shelter and fell asleep.

A woman found her there and, after talking to Audrey, she went to a kiosk and phoned the police who, of course, by that time had been alerted about her disappearance.'

'Never mind,' Sarah said, 'it's over now.'

But it wasn't over because there was still Alice.

Gareth looked in Sarah's eyes and she saw the pain in his. 'What am I going to do about Alice, Sarah?' he asked. 'What on earth am I going to do?'

'Has she admitted hurting Audrey?'

He gave a brief, harsh laugh. 'She has not! She became most upset, crying and screaming. It's a wonder you didn't hear her round here. She said I didn't love her, that I couldn't love her if I believed she was capable of doing something so horrible. She swore it was Audrey who was lying, not her, but the bruises. I'm worried about Alice, upsets like today aren't good for her. She ran out into the summerhouse and refused to come out till it started to get dark and then she was straight to bed. She won't let me into her room. So now I have two children on my hands.'

Haven't you always, Sarah thought ruefully.

She tried to say something constructive. 'Give her time.'

Gareth smiled. 'You know her so well, Sarah,' he remarked. Suddenly he looked awkward, uncomfortable, studying his well-shaped hands. 'About the weekend,' he began. 'You and . . . Tim, didn't you say?'

Sarah nodded.

Gareth went on, 'I suppose I was jealous when I saw him kissing you. I jumped to conclusions. I'm sorry.'

'But what else were you to think?' Sarah now defended him. 'You thought exactly what Tim intended you should. He's . . . very possessive.'

'Well, I'm sorry,' Gareth said again. 'I don't expect you'll see him again.'

I wouldn't bank on it, Sarah thought, but said nothing.

Was the ice being broken between them again? If so, Sarah knew she would have to tread very gently, especially now Gareth had other worries on his mind.

He moved from his chair to the sofa where Sarah was sitting, and took hold of her hand. 'When things settle down at home,' he said, 'we could go out for another meal. If you'd like to, that is.'

Sarah smiled. 'I'd like that very much,' she said.

Gareth's smile matched her own. 'Good. Now how about that offer of some tea?'

Sarah went off into the kitchen feeling so much better than she had since she found Tim Mercer on her doorstep. As she made the tea, she prayed it would be all right now. They had to make it all right. They had to trust one another, believe in one another, whatever might be lying around the corner.

7

It was July now and the weather was becoming really hot. Sometimes the heat from the hairdryers in the salon was almost unbearable and Sarah had to wedge open the door to try to let some air in. In the flat, too, she left all the windows wide open, day and night.

She saw Alice who now usually wore shorts and a gypsy top, lying on a garden lounger, or, more often, in her usual place in the summerhouse. Alice seemed fine, there had been no recriminations, no coming to Sarah's door making wild accusations. Life had continued fairly peacefully since Tim's visit and Audrey's disappearance.

She couldn't hide the truth from herself any longer. She was falling in love with Gareth.

Soon it would be the summer holidays and the question of what to do with Audrey had come up between them.

'Mrs Harmon is going to come in extra hours,' Gareth said, 'but she can't be there all the time. She has her own family. Alice will be around, of course, but she has flatly refused to be left alone with Audrey for more than a few minutes. 'I'm not going to let you have the opportunity to tell wicked lies about me again' she told me.'

So Alice was still maintaining her innocence.

'I don't mind having Audrey round here sometimes,' Sarah offered. 'She was as good as gold the first time she stayed with me. I can bring in a small table and I'm sure she's got colouring books, jigsaws and the like to keep herself amused. We can go for picnics in my lunch break perhaps.'

'Oh, Sarah.' The relief on Gareth's face was obvious. 'That would be a great help. I promise I won't burden you too much.'

Sarah laughed. 'Audrey is no burden,' she declared.

And it was true. It would be nice to have the child with her. She would be chatty and inquisitive and helpful in her own little way. Whenever she had been in the salon in the past, the customers had all taken to her, and Audrey had loved helping to serve cups of tea and biscuits to them.

'That's an enormous weight off my mind, Sarah,' Gareth said. 'My surgery seems to be overflowing at the moment and I'm sure my house calls have almost doubled. People going down with summer colds, headaches and the like. The hot weather, I suppose.'

Yes, it was certainly hot. For this reason Sarah was surprised to see Alice leaving the house one day as she was coming back from the grocery store. In the heat . . . Alice wore a full-skirted white dress, a white and pink sunhat and white gloves, carrying a small clutch bag under her arm.

She didn't see Sarah, who made quite sure she hadn't. She headed for the bus stop opposite the church and sure enough the trolley bus came up the hill from Thorley almost immediately, stopping to pick up the few passengers waiting for it, including Alice.

Now where could Alice be going? Not that it was any of her business, Sarah realised, but she knew Alice rarely strayed farther than the back garden of her home. She wondered whether Gareth was aware that his sister had left the house. He would be out on his rounds at that time and though Mrs Harmon was probably around somewhere, Audrey was not. School didn't break for the summer holidays till that weekend.

Sarah went back to the salon and during the rest of that busy day, people having their hair done before going on their annual holidays, didn't give Alice a thought. Until a couple of days later when, late in the evening, Gareth came round to see if she had seen Alice anywhere.

'No, I haven't,' Sarah told him, glad for her own sake that Gareth was there.

He was so busy that she hadn't seen much of him lately. He looked tired, she thought, as though he was under some strain.

'Mrs Harmon says she went out after lunch without saying where she was going. Mrs Harmon was very surprised because Alice never goes out, not by herself, but naturally she didn't ask any questions. She knows better than to have her head snapped off.'

Sarah decided she had better tell Gareth about Alice getting on the bus.

Gareth frowned. 'Going to town? What on earth for?'

'Shopping?' Sarah suggested.

'Alice hasn't been shopping in years. She buys all her clothes from mail order catalogues.'

'It's so unlike her,' Gareth went on. 'Of course, she's a grown woman and I don't own her, but if she overtaxes herself, there's no saying what might happen. I must admit, Sarah, I'm more than a little worried about her.'

Poor Gareth, Sarah thought. First

Audrey now Alice giving him grief. 'You know Alice,' she said lightly, but Gareth's tension did not ease.

'I've seen it happen too many times in the past, Sarah,' he said. 'She shines like a new light bulb one minute, then fades rapidly.'

Sarah didn't know what to say, so said nothing. When Gareth said, 'Anyway, it's so good to talk to you, Sarah,' she felt a warm glow spreading over her.

He got up to leave, coming towards her, putting his hands on her shoulders. 'My life's improved since you came into it,' he said softly.

His words surprised Sarah. She gave a nervous little laugh. 'What?' she cried. 'I've upset you, I've tried to deceive you, I've even been the cause of your knocking a man down.'

Gareth laughed. A good, hearty laugh that eased his tense expression.

'And very gratifying it was too,' he said.

Then he kissed her, the first passionate kiss he had given her since the first night they went out together. Sarah was sorry when it ended.

Gareth held her in his arms for a few moments. She felt safe there.

'If only it was just you and me,' he said longingly.

But it wasn't and it never would be. Sarah drew away from him.

'I suppose I'd better go,' Gareth said.

Alone again, Sarah felt restless. Would it always be like this? Snatched moments, seeing one another only fleetingly.

On Saturday morning, Sarah was drawing back her living room curtains when she saw Alice coming out through the french windows. Alice looked up and saw her and gave a cheery wave. At least I seem to be in her good books, Sarah thought. As the windows were already open to their fullest, Sarah could hear plainly when Alice called out:

'Come round when the salon's closed. I want to talk to you. Gareth's taking Audrey shopping in town in a few minutes and they'll be away most of the day.'

So no chance of catching a glimpse of him then. Sarah wasn't at all sure she wanted to visit Alice, but she leaned out of the window.

'All right,' she said, 'I'll be round after lunch.'

Alice seemed full of suppressed excitement. Her eyes were bright, her movements jerky. There was something brittle about her.

'Come into the sitting room,' she said, grabbing hold of Sarah's arm in that possessive way she had. 'It's cool in there at this time of day. Mrs Harmon's gone home but she's left some things for tea.'

'I'm not hungry,' Sarah told her.

'Maybe later then.' Alice smiled.

Like a cat that's been at the cream, Sarah thought as she watched Alice curl up in her usual position on the sofa, looking out through half-closed eyelids.

'What's the matter?' Sarah asked. 'You seem . . . ' She couldn't think of the right word to use.

Alice laughed. 'I'm in love,' she cried.

That wasn't what Sarah had expected to hear. 'Oh, my,' Alice went on, 'you do look surprised. Do you think you're the only one who can fall in love?'

Sarah looked down at her hands. Another unexpected remark.

'Oh, Sarah, you're so transparent. It's so obvious, every time my brother is around.'

Sarah felt on edge. 'You sound as though you don't mind,' she said, not bothering to deny anything.

'Why should I mind?'

'Well, you did say to me that you and Gareth . . . '

Alice broke in, 'That was me being selfish. Don't take any notice of me. I'm pleased for Gareth, really I am.'

Why don't I believe her, Sarah thought?

'And now, I've met somebody of my own so I can appreciate how you feel, Sarah.'

'Someone Gareth knows?' Sarah asked warily.

Alice's eyes narrowed. 'Of course not, and you mustn't tell him. He won't approve. Oh, he wants me to approve of what he does, but when it comes to myself, well, that's an entirely different matter. He'll say I'm not well enough, not strong enough but that's nonsense.' She stretched her arms above her head in a cat-like movement. 'I've never felt better in my life!'

She did seem to have energy, but Sarah remembered what Gareth had said about his sister being bright and full of life one minute, and drained and ill the next.

'So are you going to tell me who this new friend is?' she asked pleasantly.

Alice shook her head. 'Ah, that's a secret.'

Sarah suddenly had an alarming suspicion that the man in question might be married. It was obvious that he was the person Alice had gone to meet when she got the bus to town, and had been seeing the night Gareth came round because she wasn't home.

'Not even his name?' Sarah prompted.

'Not just yet. In time.' Alice got up and danced around the room.

'Does he know about your . . . ' She couldn't finish the sentence.

Alice came to a halt in front of her. 'About my illness?' she snapped. 'That's what you were going to say, isn't it? No, he doesn't. I shall tell him in my own good time. Oh, Sarah, you've spoiled things now. I was so excited I just had to tell somebody and who else was there but you? Mrs Harmon? Audrey?' She scowled. 'I don't think so.'

Sarah felt mean. 'I can see whoever it is, he's made you very happy,' she said, thinking of how she felt about Gareth. How could she begrudge Alice who was, after all, twenty-four, just as she was, the need to fall in love and to be loved?

But it was all so sudden and she had to ask, 'How did you meet him, Alice?'

Alice giggled. 'It was silly, really. I was in the front garden and he drove past in his car and stopped to ask me for directions. We started talking. I was alone in the house and he came into the front garden and we sat on the bench under the window. We talked for ages. You know how I am with strangers but I wasn't like that with him. If you'd been around, Sarah, you would have seen us together.'

But she hadn't been around and suddenly a terrible suspicion dropped into Sarah's mind.

'Is he called Tim?' she asked.

'Tim? Why, no, what makes you ask that?' Alice cried.

Sarah laughed. 'A wild guess,' she said.

Alice didn't look convinced. 'No, nothing like that,' she said. 'I suppose I can tell you. It's Mark. But that's all I am telling you. Now, remember, not a word to Gareth. Promise me!'

Sarah reluctantly gave her word even though she knew Gareth would be angry if he found out later that she had known about this Mark before he did. But why should he be angry? He wasn't a Dickensian father, he was merely an older brother, a protective brother it was true, but Alice was entitled to happiness just like everybody else.

For the time being Sarah had no choice but to keep Alice's news to herself. If the new man in Alice's life was worth anything, he would no doubt be a visitor at The White House before long. If not, and it all blew over, as well it might, there was no need for Gareth to be any the wiser.

It was Gareth himself who brought Audrey round to the salon on Monday morning.

She settled Audrey at the small table she had brought down from the flat and walked outside with Gareth.

'Is everything all right?' she asked quietly. 'With Audrey, I mean?'

'Yes, I think so, especially since she received a letter from her mother the other day.'

'Really? I didn't know your cousin was well enough for that.'

'Apparently so. I spoke to her doctor

incidentally at the weekend. They've reassessed her condition and she isn't as bad as they first feared. They're talking more medium term care than long term now, thank God.'

Good news, indeed. Sarah glanced round to where Audrey was bending over her colouring book, her shiny hair flopping over her face, her tongue between her lips as she concentrated.

Gareth went on, 'Audrey was thrilled with the letter. I think she's got it with her to show you.'

'I look forward to reading it,' Sarah said.

She was surprised but pleased when Gareth bent and kissed her cheek. 'Another busy day ahead of me,' he said. 'I'm on my way to visit two young children. They're not very well, I'm afraid. Different families but both sick and complaining of head and neck pains.' He looked up at the azure sky. Even at nine o'clock in the morning the air was hot and stifling. 'I blame this heat. We could do with a downpour to cool it down.'

'Don't say that,' Sarah protested, 'the summer's only just got under way. We don't want rain.'

'Maybe not.' Gareth grinned.

He walked to his car which was parked at the kerb and turned to give Sarah a cheery wave before he drove off. Dreamily, she stood watching him, only going inside when he disappeared at the end of the street. She had a good feeling about how things were going with Gareth.

There hadn't been a cross word between them for ages. Of course, she reminded herself, Alice's mysterious beau still hovered in the background, but she wasn't going to allow that to spoil things.

Audrey looked up. She reached inside one of the books she had brought along and produced a white envelope.

'Here.' She thrust it at Sarah. 'It's a letter from my mummy and you can read it if you want.'

Sarah took the envelope from her. She was aware that the child was watching her intently as she read from the single sheet of paper.

It was written in a clear and beautiful style of handwriting. The wording was poignant, by a mother to a little girl, with deep feeling but so that a ten-year-old child could understand. A well thought out letter from an educated person and Sarah was ashamed to feel surprise because, maybe due to Alice's description of Edith's life and background, she had imagined her to be of poor education, struggling alone to bring up her daughter, battling against mental health problems and poverty.

Here was a caring mother whose ability to compose such a letter under such circumstances must surely be a credit to her.

Sarah carefully re-folded the sheet of paper, replaced it in the envelope and handed it back to Audrey.

'Thank you, Audrey,' she said softly, 'for letting me read it.'

Audrey grinned. 'My mummy's sick,

you know,' she said, 'but she'll be coming home soon. She says so, doesn't she?'

'Yes, she does.' Sarah felt sure Edith would not give Audrey hope if there was none.

Sarah went over and put her arms around Audrey, holding her close.

Gareth came back just as Sarah was closing the salon. She had been wondering whether she ought to take Audrey round to The White House, but hesitated to do so in case Alice was there alone. Alternatively, she could have taken Audrey upstairs with her and given her something to eat, but now it wouldn't be necessary.

'Gareth's here,' she said to Audrey as she saw him getting out of his car.

'I can give him my drawing, can't I?' She beamed. 'He can hang it in his surgery.'

Sarah didn't answer, distracted by the expression on Gareth's face. He had seen her but there was no wave of the hand, no smile. Her heart felt heavy, dreading to hear what was wrong now, thinking only that it must have something to do with Alice. Or her.

She went to the open doorway. 'Hello,' she greeted with a brightness she did not feel.

'Those children,' he said. 'I know what's wrong with them now. There have already been two other confirmed cases.'

'What?' Sarah prompted.

Gareth looked into her eyes, and she saw the fear in his.

'Polio.'

8

Poliomyelitis. A word that struck terror into every parent's heart. That evening, quite late, Gareth took Sarah across to The Bell Inn. Neither of them had been in before and were quite impressed by its olde worlde interior and its comfortable upholstered benches set in nooks and crannies, so affording the maximum of privacy should you want it.

Mrs Harmon had agreed to come in and sit with Audrey, and they had waited until the child was in bed and asleep before going out. Alice, too, had retired early. Gareth told Sarah she had been out for most of the afternoon and was exhausted.

'I can't understand her,' he said, 'where on earth does she go that she needs to be so secretive about it?'

Sarah realised that it would never cross Gareth's mind in a month of

Sundays that his sister was seeing someone and she found this rather sad. Most older brothers would tease a sister who started to be secretive about her comings and goings. She was glad when Gareth, as she had known he would, started to talk about the outbreak of that terrible disease. It meant she had did not have to wonder whether she should tell him what she knew about Alice.

'They've already closed the swimming pool,' he said.

'Oh, what a shame,' Sarah cried. 'Is that really necessary? I mean the summer holidays have only just started.'

Gareth stared at her. 'Vital. Indeed anywhere that young people congregate in large numbers must be carefully controlled.'

'Of course,' Sarah felt ashamed of her ignorance.

There had been outbreaks when she was growing up, but she had never known anyone personally who had succumbed to the disease. Whilst

Gareth, of course, must have seen its ravages at first hand.

He took a long drink from his pint glass. 'I needed that,' he told her with a weary smile.

'There is a vaccination programme now, isn't there?' she queried.

'Yes, but unfortunately until there is an outbreak of the disease a great many people shy away from vaccination. A head in the sand attitude I expect.'

Gareth went on, 'And at the moment vaccination is limited to children, not young adults, though they can be vulnerable to attack as well. Also, once the disease is active then, it's often too late for preventative treatment. By then, it's more or less a waiting game, seeing how far the disease will progress.'

'Is it always bad news?'

'Not always. Sometimes the paralysis can be superficial, with little or no permanent impairment. At other times . . . ' he shrugged his shoulders, 'there is considerable damage, and, of course, even death.'

Sarah found herself shivering. 'And those terrible iron lungs,' she said.

Gareth smiled. 'Or to give them their correct name, tank respirators.' He took another drink and Sarah sipped from her orange juice. 'Nowadays, though, progress has been made and tracheotomy is often used, the inserting of a breathing tube into the throat. Brought about, as is often the case, by necessity. You see, in 1952, there was a massive epidemic in Copenhagen and they were literally running out of respirators.'

Sarah looked at Gareth with admiration. 'You're obviously very well read,' she said.

'I am a doctor,' he said modestly. 'Anyway, we must be optimistic. Only time will tell if the disease is showing up in other towns and cities. We may be lucky, if you can call it luck, and be able to contain it here.'

But that optimism proved to be unfounded and the disease continued to manifest itself, with more and more young people showing symptoms. Queues began to form outside clinics as desperate people brought their children for the oral sugar lump vaccination. As a single doctor practice, Gareth was rushed off his feet, day and night. He had volunteered to do his stint at the local hospital, sometimes staying there all night, then going straight to his own surgery the next morning.

When Sarah saw him she was shocked by his appearance. Often he didn't even have time to shave and his eyes were red-rimmed and hollow. Sarah knew, too, he was worried sick about Audrey, though, despite her protests, she had been vaccinated.

Sarah had the child with her often now, to make things easier both for Mrs Harmon and Gareth, as Alice continued to float around in a dream-like state, often away from the house, obviously with her friend, Mark, who-ever he may be, and totally oblivious to the epidemic raging around her.

Sarah kept a cautious eye on Audrey, alert for any signs of aches and pains, but, thank goodness, Audrey continued in robust good health, though she was a bit put out when Sarah didn't want to take her to the park and swings as they had been used to doing.

She had made friends there and she missed them. Sarah was sure she would not be the only person to keep children away from parks and playgrounds. You could never be too careful, and she spent as much time as she could, making it up to Audrey, playing games with her, letting her help more in the salon, though she did wonder if Audrey's ears took in more than they should of the general discussion about polio.

To begin with, the news on the wireless and in the papers was gloomy, but as the weeks passed, it did seem that the epidemic was starting to wane, with fewer and fewer new cases being reported. The pressure on Gareth and other dedicated doctors started to ease.

During this time, Sarah and Gareth found themselves drawing closer and closer together. Finally, one night when they returned from one of their late walks up the fields — occasions they both needed and appreciated — Gareth told Sarah he loved her.

He took her in his arms for their usual goodnight kiss, but kept her close against him for a long time.

'Thank you, Sarah,' he said softly.

When he released her, he took hold of her hands. 'I love you, Sarah. Will you marry me?'

Her heart missed a beat. Before she flung her arms around his neck and cried, 'Yes, oh, yes,' she urged herself to be cautious.

'Is . . . is it the right time?' she asked. 'Shouldn't we wait?'

'Is any time the right time? And yes, it's true, we should wait, and we will. Till the epidemic is well and truly over. But that doesn't stop your agreeing to be my wife. In saying you love me too.'

She kissed his lips gently. 'I think you know I do,' she said. 'But,' here came the voice of caution, 'what about Alice?

What about Audrey?'

'Well, Audrey will be delighted, I'm sure, to be a bridesmaid.'

'And Alice?' Sarah prompted.

'Seems to have found a life of her own. I wish she'd be more open about it, but I won't force her. So long as I keep a close eye on her condition, and make sure she visits her own doctor for regular check ups, Alice shouldn't be a problem.'

But Sarah hadn't meant just her state of health. Alice could react to the news that she and Gareth were engaged, in one of two ways. She could be absolutely delighted. Or she could fly into a rage as she had when Audrey was coming to stay. No one could be certain which way she would go.

Another thing, Sarah knew this was a perfect opportunity to tell Gareth about 'Mark', but she still held back. She had given her word. She needed to talk to Alice first before she spoke.

Gareth grinned. 'You're taking an awfully long time to say 'yes',' he teased.

Sarah took a deep breath, casting doubts and worries aside. 'Yes, I will marry you, Dr Bradley, thank you for asking me,' she said.

They decided they would tell Alice immediately. It was late, but through the uncurtained windows of The White House sitting-room, they could see Alice walking about, ready for bed in her dressing-gown it was true, but not yet having gone upstairs.

They walked into the sitting-room hand-in-hand. Alice turned from where she had been looking at herself in the mirror above the fireplace. She started to say, 'So you do come home sometimes, Gareth,' when she saw he was not alone. 'Ah, Sarah,' she went on, and her eyes strayed to their clasped hands.

Before she could say anything else Gareth said, 'I've asked Sarah to marry me, and she's said she will.'

For a moment Sarah thought Alice was going to say something hurtful, something spiteful as her eyes narrowed and her lips compressed. Then she recovered herself.

'Why, that's wonderful!' she cried.

She came forward and kissed them both on the cheek. 'Congratulations to you both. When's the happy day to be?'

'We haven't decided on a date yet,' Gareth told her. He glanced at Sarah. 'Some time in the autumn perhaps?'

Sarah nodded.

'Lovely!' She took hold of both Sarah's hands in a sisterly gesture and lead her to the sofa where they both sat down whilst Gareth seemed to hover in the background. 'No ring yet, of course,' she lifted Sarah's left hand. 'You must get him to buy you a very expensive ring, Sarah.'

'Don't worry, I will,' Sarah said with a smile, entering into the spirit of the thing.

Alice looked up at Gareth. 'We must have a celebratory drink,' she declared. 'What have we got?'

'Not much,' Gareth admitted, eyeing their depleted drinks trolley woefully. Once Audrey came to live with them, alcoholic drink of any kind had been removed for safety reasons.

'I'd as soon have a cup of tea as anything stronger,' Sarah said.

'That won't do at all,' Alice said reprovingly. 'Gareth go and see what you can find. Surely there must be something in the kitchen. But, for goodness sake don't bring Mrs Harmon's dreadful cooking sherry.'

Gareth dutifully did as he was told and left the room and Sarah waited for the vitriol to appear. But she was wrong. Alice took hold of her hands once more and her face was alight with happiness.

'I'm so pleased, Sarah,' she cried. 'I'll have a sister-in-law and you can come and live here and look after Gareth, and ease some of the pressure on me.'

Sarah couldn't believe what she was hearing. But Alice must have seen the expression in her eyes because she rushed on. 'Oh, I know Gareth tries to make out I'm the one who needs looking after, but its simply not true.

Well, look at me.' She held out her arms. 'Don't you think I'm looking extremely well these days?'

Yes, she was, but wasn't she a bit too excited, didn't she have a sort of feverish glint in her pale blue eyes?

Alice leaned forward conspiratorially. 'That's because I'm in love,' she whispered, 'and now, because of you and Gareth, I can tell Gareth about Mark.'

'You'll tell him tonight?' Sarah asked.

'No. Tomorrow. When he and I are alone.'

But Sarah wondered if she really would. Once again, with that evasive look she used so expertly, Alice's eyes had slid away from Sarah's as she answered.

Gareth returned and Alice became the attentive hostess, handing Sarah a glass of sherry she didn't really want.

'Not Mrs Harmon's cooking sherry,' was Alice's assurance.

From then until Sarah left about half-an-hour later, Alice dominated the conversation. She seemed to have it all planned out, Sarah and Gareth's wedding, what Sarah should wear, what she, Alice, should wear as chief bridesmaid. Even the flowers.

Sarah couldn't bring herself to put a halt to Alice's flow of excited chatter, mainly because early on, she had caught Gareth's eye and he seemed to be saying, 'Let her have her head.'

But then, all of a sudden, Alice seemed to flag. She put a hand to her forehead. 'Alice?' Gareth said sharply, 'Are you all right?'

'A little tired, I think.'

Automatically Gareth caught hold of his sister's wrist, and seemed to be checking her pulse, but Alice pulled sharply free.

'We don't want to play doctors, Gareth,' she snapped. 'I'm all right.' And she got rather unsteadily to her feet.

She held out her arms to Sarah and Sarah moved into Alice's embrace. It was the first time Alice had ever held her and she was shocked to discover how thin and frail Alice felt.

'Goodnight, dear Sarah,' Alice said, 'I shall dream of wedding cake and orange blossoms tonight.'

And, after kissing Gareth, she drifted out of the room, leaving Sarah feeling distinctly uneasy.

Alice was plotting something, she felt sure of it. But what?

The next day, Alice had gone. Sarah had had a telephone installed in the salon the week before, after having to wait, it seemed for ages, and when it rang in the middle of the afternoon, she presumed it was a potential customer and put on her 'salon' voice.

'Good afternoon, Pink Ribbon Salon. May I help you?'

'Sarah?' It was Gareth. Just the one word but it was enough for Sarah to be alert to what might be coming next.

'What is it, Gareth?' she asked.

Audrey, busy sweeping the floor stopped in her work to watch and listen.

'It's Alice. Can you come round? I can't leave the house, I'm expecting an important phone call any minute.'

'Is she ill?'

'Please, Sarah,' and Gareth put the phone down.

At the moment Sarah was between customers but she was expecting the next one in fifteen minutes which, to her mind, made it as important for her not to leave the salon as it was for Gareth not to leave the house. But she took Audrey with her and she went round anyway, thinking it had better be something worthwhile and not one of Alice's tantrums.

As soon as Gareth opened the door he said, 'Audrey?' as though disappointed she was there.

'I couldn't leave her, Gareth,' Sarah told him.

'No, of course you couldn't.' Gareth turned to the child. 'Run into the kitchen, Audrey, Mrs Harmon will give you a drink and a biscuit.'

Audrey seemed delighted at the

prospect, and well she might be, as Sarah had only just given her a snack a few minutes ago.

When they were alone, Sarah said, 'What's the matter with Alice now?'

'She's gone.'

'Gone? What do you mean she's gone?'

Gareth passed her a piece of pink writing paper.

'She left this on the mantelpiece. She must have gone whilst I was in the surgery and Mrs Harmon elsewhere. Simply sneaked out. Read it.'

He sat down abruptly and Sarah read the brief note.

Dear Gareth, I'm going away. Don't worry about me I shall be fine. Mark will look after me. We shall probably get married, but I'll be in touch as soon as I know anything definite. Love, Alice. PS I've taken all my medication with me.

Before Sarah could make any comment, Gareth spoke in an angry, frustrated voice. 'Who's this Mark, for goodness' sake? I didn't know she was seeing anyone. What can she be thinking of? At least this explains why she was so mysterious and continually away from the house. I can tell you, Sarah, I'm out of my mind with worry.'

'I'm sure she'll be all right, Gareth,' Sarah said, feeling very guilty now about the secret she had kept.

'But who is this Mark chap?' he repeated. 'Do you know anything about him?'

The direct question threw Sarah and she felt herself blushing. Gareth looked closely at her.

'You do, don't you?' he challenged.

So she had no choice but to tell him what she knew.

He exploded into anger. Apart from the time he crossed swords with Tim Mercer, Sarah had never seen Gareth angry, but now she realised that when driven he was capable of it and she trembled, sitting down as far away from him as she could.

'Were you keeping a secret with my

sister? Knowing full well how delicate her state of health was and you didn't see fit to tell me?'

'Alice made me promise. I wasn't happy about it but what could I do?'

Suddenly Gareth looked deflated. He ran his hands over his face. 'Nothing, I suppose,' he said, 'when you put it like that.'

Encouraged by his change of mood, Sarah went and sat by him on the sofa, touching his arm gently.

'I'm sorry, Gareth, but you must know how persuasive Alice can be.'

He gave a weak smile. 'Don't I just?' he agreed.

'She'll be in touch, I'm sure,' though she wasn't.

'She's talking of marrying. Marrying! Does the man know about her health problems?'

The phone rang at that moment and Gareth excused himself and left the room. He must have gone into the surgery because Sarah couldn't hear him speaking from the hall. He was gone quite a few minutes. Sarah listened to Mrs Harmon and Audrey laughing in the kitchen. No doubt young Audrey would be sampling more of the housekeeper's wares whilst she had the chance.

She recalled the excited, secretive look on Alice's face the night before. Had she already decided to leave home, or had it been a spur of the moment decision because of Sarah and Gareth's engagement? Had she had an opportunity to contact her boyfriend, and arrange for him to pick her up? It was typical of Alice that she would do exactly what she wanted and not give a thought to her brother's anguish over her.

Gareth returned. 'I'm sorry, Sarah,' he said, 'but I've got to go out.' He came and kissed her. 'I'm sorry as well that I flew off the handle.'

She touched his cheek gently. 'I know how you must be feeling, what are you going to do now?'

He shrugged. 'Heaven only knows.

Wait for Alice to come to her senses and come home, I suppose.'

'And if she doesn't?' Sarah couldn't help herself from saying, 'Where does that leave you and me?'

Gareth laughed. 'You silly girl,' he admonished gently, 'do you think I'd let Alice's pranks come between us? On Saturday we're going out to buy that ring, come hell or high water.'

She should have been over the moon by those words but instead her mind refused to move away from Alice.

9

Alice did not contact Gareth. No letter, no phone call. As the poliomyelitis epidemic continued throughout the country, though encouragingly still on the wane, Sarah knew how desperate Gareth was for some news of his sister's whereabouts and safety, but there was nothing either of them could do, so they got on with their lives as best they could.

They took the promised trip into Heaton, scouring jewellers' windows for a suitable engagement ring. Sarah was astounded at some of the prices.

'That's rather nice,' Gareth said, pointing to a very large solitaire diamond.

'Have you seen how much it costs?' Sarah cried.

'Let me worry about the price,' Gareth told her. He grinned. 'On the other hand, perhaps that particular one would break the bank.'

'I should think so indeed,' Sarah reproved.

Choosing a ring together, actually being in town together, having lunch, browsing, was such a pleasant experience that for a short while at least Sarah and Gareth need think only of themselves.

The weather had cooled slightly, still remaining warm and sunny but not so oppressive. Audrey was in Mrs Harmon's safe hands. The housekeeper's youngest child was having a birthday party and Audrey, to her delight, had been invited. It was to be only a small party, Mrs Harmon had expressed worries at having too many children in the house at one time because of the epidemic, though Gareth had tried to assure her there would be no danger there.

He had taken Audrey, wearing her new pink and white party dress, round to Mrs Harmon's and she was also going to spend the night there, another special treat.

Gareth had remarked to Sarah. 'Audrey's come a long way, hasn't she, since she first came here?'

Mrs Harmon had told them, 'Now you two go off and enjoy yourselves. Buy Sarah a lovely ring, Doctor. And don't you worry about Audrey, I'll look after her as though she was my own.'

It was nice, exciting to be spending so much time together, talking about their wedding, making plans, and they did go out that evening, Sarah pleased to be showing off her new ring, unable to stop looking at it as it sparkled on her finger, placed there solemnly by Gareth. It was hard to believe that they would soon be man and wife. They had decided that, whatever was the outcome of Alice's little escapade, they would get married in the middle of October.

Gareth was optimistic then that the polio scare would be almost over. His workload would ease and they would be able to think about a honeymoon.

'And, of course,' he said, leaning across the table to take hold of Sarah's hand, 'I'm sure Alice will be back by then.'

'Of course she will,' Sarah agreed, but to be honest, she did not really share Gareth's confidence, and wondered briefly if indeed he was as confident as he sounded.

She hoped Alice would come home, of course she did, but if Alice didn't see fit to even let Gareth know where she was, and she was enjoying her freedom and being in love, maybe even thinking of getting married herself, after all she had hinted at that, they would just have to go ahead with their own arrangements.

'Shall we get married in Thorley?' Gareth asked, picking up his spoon to start on the dessert the waiter had just put before him. 'It's a lovely little church.'

'But there's one just across the road,' Sarah pointed out.

'Yes, I know, but have you ever been inside it?'

Sarah had to admit that she had not.

'Well I have. To a wedding, as it happens. It's a great big barn of a place. Cold, no matter how many heaters they put on, gloomy, far too big.'

Sarah laughed. 'All right, you've proved your point.'

'Whereas St Paul's church in Thorley is reminiscent of a real country church, in a small well-kept graveyard, no falling down tombstones as at St John's, there's even a stream running along side it and a swathe of lawn, perfect for wedding pictures.'

'Sounds wonderful! We'd better go and see the vicar as soon as possible, before he gets booked up.'

'How about going to service tomorrow? I supposed we'd better show willing if we want the church's blessing on our marriage.'

Sarah was more than happy to go along with that. She wasn't a regular attender but she was a believer and had been both christened and confirmed into the Church of England.

It was dark as they drove home in companionable silence. Sarah was thinking of Mrs Harmon's words. The White House would be empty, really empty for the first time since she had known Gareth. No Alice. No Audrey. Just her and Gareth. Would he invite her in? Maybe for a coffee, even though they had taken coffee at the restaurant.

Instead of driving round and parking by the salon, as he usually did, Gareth turned straight into his driveway and Sarah caught her breath.

'I suppose the night is still young,' Gareth remarked, turning off the ignition.

'Yes.'

He leaned forward to kiss her lips and she put her arms around his neck, there in the warm darkness of the car's interior. But the spell was broken when someone rapped sharply on the side window.

They both drew apart. Gareth peered out. 'Edith!' he gasped, leaping out of the car, gathering the shadowy figure of a tall woman into his arms.

Sarah climbed out of her side and stood there, awkward, embarrassed.

Gareth released the woman and turned to Sarah.

'Sarah, this is my cousin, Edith Bailey. Edith, this is Sarah, my fiancée. Actually we just got engaged today.'

Edith smiled. 'Congratulations,' she said, 'to you both.'

She and Sarah shook hands. Edith's fingers were cool.

Her appearance was a total surprise to Sarah. She had ascertained from the letter she wrote to Audrey, that Edith was an educated woman, but she had not been prepared for someone of such beauty, with a deep, well-modulated voice. Thick dark hair fell to her shoulders. Her eyes were almond shaped, her mouth generous. She was wearing a dark coat with the collar turned up at the back and was easily as tall as Gareth.

But the remarkable thing was that she looked so well. No sign of strain or

151

illness, no edginess or tiredness that Alice frequently displayed. Totally calm and relaxed.

'Well,' Gareth cried, 'let's get inside.' He produced his key and opened the door, switching on the hall light. 'Edith, what on earth are you doing here? Not absconded, have you?'

Edith laughed delightedly. 'Of course not. I'm free, Gareth. Out for good. Aren't you pleased?'

'You know I am.' Once in the sitting room Gareth held out his arms again to his cousin and she came into them so naturally that Sarah began to feel out of things.

'But at this time of night? They can't possibly have released you so late.'

Edith removed her coat. Underneath she wore a slinky dark blue dress with a single string of pearls around her neck. She had long, elegant legs. She was wearing make up, carefully applied. She resembled a fashion model more than she did a woman who had just been released from a mental home.

'I left Leeds at lunch time,' she said. 'I phoned you several times before I did so, but there was no reply. My doctor tried to get hold of you as well, but to no avail. Of course, Gareth, before you remind me of the fact, I know you are a busy doctor and what with this wretched polio epidemic . . . '

For the first time Edith showed signs of distress, looking down at her hands, twisting them together.

Gareth went and sat by her on the sofa and Sarah, feeling distinctly like an interloper, took an armchair.

'And you were worried about Audrey, is that it?' Gareth asked gently.

Edith nodded without speaking.

Gareth patted Edith's fingers. 'Then don't be. She's fine, full of health and vitality. She's staying at a friend's house tonight. Won't she be thrilled when she comes back and finds you here? But, tell me, Edith, how is it you are here? Did you discharge yourself?'

Edith looked into Gareth's eyes. 'I was a voluntary patient, Gareth and was free to leave whenever I wished. I thought you understood that.'

'No, I was never given very much detail, don't ask me why, you would have thought with my being a doctor . . . '

'Anyway, I'm here,' Edith broke in. 'I'm well. I feel one hundred per cent better than I did. There had been pressures, I'd been ill with flu, we had money worries . . . '

'Why didn't you contact me earlier?' Gareth scolded. 'I would have helped you, you know that.'

Edith smiled. 'I know. But you have Alice, and that's enough for any man.' She looked around. 'Where is Alice by the way? I was surprised the house was empty when I got here. I went for a walk and then I just . . . hung around I suppose, waiting for you to come back.'

'Alice is out too,' Gareth said and for the first time he glanced at Sarah with an expression that said quite clearly, 'Let's leave Alice out of this, shall we?'

Edith too looked at Sarah. 'I'm sorry,

Sarah,' she apologised, 'you must think Gareth and I are very rude. Especially when you've just become engaged. May I see your ring?'

Sarah held out her hand. 'It's beautiful. You're a very lucky man, Gareth.'

'I know,' and Gareth got up and moved to Sarah's chair, sitting on the arm, placing his arm gently around her shoulders.

'I shall want to know all about how you two met, every last detail, but just now I'm dying for a cup of tea. The stuff they served in that hospital couldn't possibly be called tea.'

Sarah stood up. 'Let me make it,' she said.

She half-hoped Gareth would say, 'I'll help you,' but he didn't.

She could hear them talking quietly, and laughing and she couldn't stop a feeling of acute jealousy. This was to have been a special time for her and Gareth, a rare moment together, now Gareth and his cousin would be sleeping under the same roof, no doubt chatting far into the night once she had gone home.

She was being unreasonable, she knew, but couldn't stop herself. Poor Edith, being shut away in a hospital ward, taking pills, undergoing gruelling therapy perhaps, parted from her child. But the thing was, Edith didn't seem in any way like a victim. She had talked quite freely in front of Sarah about her problems, almost as though Sarah wasn't there.

But when Sarah went back into the sitting room with the tea, things changed. The intimacy that seemed to have sprung up between Gareth and Edith vanished, and Sarah's confidence grew as Gareth by every word and gesture made it plain that he loved her. Oh, he loved Edith too, but in a completely different way.

Sarah warmed to Edith, finding her easy to talk to, also a good listener. Whatever demons had possessed her, they were there no more. Here was a happy, well-balanced woman, eager to resume contact with her daughter, excited at the prospect.

'I'm considering moving here,' Edith said as she sipped her tea. She had taken off her shoes and stretched out her feet in their sheer silk stockings. 'If, as you say, Gareth, Audrey is doing well at school, I don't really want to upheave her again. When she's eleven she'll have to change schools anyway and I think that will be enough to be going on with, though. She's bright and intelligent and I'm sure she'll do well.

'I need my family around me, such as it is,' she smiled a little sadly as she said this. 'It was wrong of me to shut myself away in that awful flat all these years. Audrey deserves better.'

'I'll use all the influence I have, Edith, to help you find another place,' Gareth said, 'if that's what you want.'

'That's kind of you,' Edith said, 'but I want to be able to pay my own way. Get a job . . . stop feeling sorry for myself.' She seemed to shake off the serious mood that had overtaken her. 'Sarah, will you do something with my hair?' she declared, running her fingers through it.

'Not cut it off surely,' Sarah cried, vividly remembering the first time she had met Alice in the salon.

'No, but perhaps thin it out a bit; condition it.'

'I'd be delighted.'

'Thank you.' Edith smiled.

She had a lovely face, Sarah thought.

It was very late when finally Gareth walked her round to the flat, having left Edith making up her bed in the spare bedroom. It was a good job, Sarah thought, that The White House had four bedrooms. Enough for everybody when she and Gareth got married. She tried not to think that Edith might take ages to find a place for herself and Audrey.

'Thank you for being so understanding, Sarah,' Gareth said, kissing her.

'She's beautiful, your cousin, isn't she?'

'Very,' Gareth agreed. 'She was very well educated, university and all that. But she made a bad marriage and had Audrey when she was quite young. She was also fiercely independent. She once said to me, years ago, 'I've made my bed so I'll have to lie on it.' And this is what she did. Before he died, her husband had used up all Edith's money, gambling and drinking and they had to move to a flat in a poor area. They never got out of it.'

Sarah remembered Alice telling her a similar story, but without the sympathy and understanding.

She smiled at Gareth. 'Edith's lucky to have you,' she whispered.

'And I'm more than lucky to have you, darling,' Gareth replied. 'And don't worry about our plans, our wedding will go ahead no matter what. I'll find Edith somewhere to live, I'll have to be discreet, of course, she won't want it to look like charity, but she'll be in her own place before the wedding.'

Sarah had to be content with that,

but she still spent a restless night. So much seemed to be happening to her since she moved to her new home. Most of it good, of course, and she hoped that once Edith and Audrey were settled in a place of their own, they too, would be able to find some of the happiness she and Gareth had.

Sarah stood watching Edith and Audrey in the garden. The child was shrieking with laughter as they played a makeshift game of tennis. Edith had tied back her long hair with a red ribbon, just like Audrey's ribbon, and was wearing a gaily patterned dirndl skirt and a white blouse. Sarah had noticed the small suitcase she had brought with her, but was rather surprised that Edith had such nice clothes. Seconds later she was chiding herself for her uncharitable thoughts.

Edith's clothes might be far from new; she might be a very careful person as far as clothing was concerned. And those beautiful pearls she wore could have been a legacy.

So, now mother and daughter were re-united and from then on Audrey was no longer such a frequent visitor to the salon. Why should she be? She had her mummy and, once again, Sarah experienced an unreasonable feeling of jealousy. She had been imagining that when she and Gareth were married, they would be able to raise Audrey together.

But as the days went by she had more or less accepted Edith's presence. She was such a friendly, out-going person, eager to please and helpful. She had made an instant friend of Mrs Harmon who seemed willing to let Edith help in the kitchen, an area she usually guarded so jealously.

When Gareth told Sarah that he had checked with the hospital about Edith's discharge, she was shocked.

'You shouldn't have done that,' she cried.

'I only had Edith's welfare at heart. What she doesn't know can't hurt her and it was true what she said, she was perfectly free to leave whenever she wanted and the doctor assured me that he was quite happy for her to do so. She'll be going back to see him in four weeks. I've seen her appointment card on the kitchen shelf, so she's made no secret of it.'

Sarah felt confident that, whatever had caused Edith's breakdown, she was fully recovered now. Having witnessed Alice's strange behaviour, she had no fears about Edith's future.

She and Gareth went to see the vicar of St Paul's, a small fussy man with a likeable manner and a friendly welcome. He was more than happy to marry them. It turned out that Gareth was his sister-in-law's doctor and that seemed to be all the endorsement he needed.

So the wedding was fixed, the arrangements were in hand, Audrey was the happiest little girl in the world and it seemed that Edith's place of her own was just around the corner with the offer of a small rented cottage in

Thorley village, an ideal spot because it was close to Audrey's school.

There also seemed to be an opening in the local florist's shop and though Edith laughingly declared she had never worked in a shop she was more than willing to give it a try.

The only blot on the horizon was Alice. Or at least the lack of any news from her. Edith had been told all about Alice's escapade and her advice to Gareth was, 'Let her be. It's a few years since I saw Alice but she isn't the sort of person you'd forget. Give her her head and she'll come home, not like the prodigal daughter I'm quite sure, but all in one piece. She's a grown woman, Gareth, she must be allowed to stand on her own feet, and make her own decisions, no matter what the state of her health.'

Sarah had a feeling that Edith believed Alice's health problems were somewhat exaggerated, which seemed a little odd knowing what she herself had just been through.

At the end of September, the weather changed drastically, it started to rain and it seemed it would never want to stop. Sarah hoped it would improve by her wedding day. The good news was, no more cases of polio had been recorded for nearly a week and most of the victims in this particular epidemic were not severely crippled.

Sarah lay in bed one night, thinking about her wedding, listening to the rain pattering on the windows. She had already bought her dress which was hanging in the wardrobe alongside Audrey's little dress. The child had insisted Sarah hide it away with her own, so no-one would see it till the big day.

Sarah had made arrangements for her mother to be brought to the church. She may not be well enough to attend the reception afterwards, but Sarah was determined she should see her only child get married. It might be that Mrs Mallinson wouldn't really know what was going on; on the other hand, if she was having a good day, she might be able to understand and Sarah didn't want her mother to miss that opportunity.

Beginning to drift into sleep, a loud knocking on the street door brought her fully awake.

She sat up in bed. Was it thundering? But no, the knocking came again and Sarah got her dressing gown and ran down the stairs. It could only be bad news, why else would someone come to the door at this time of night? She feverishly unbolted and unlocked the door and flung it open.

Standing like a drowned rat on the doorstep, his hands hanging by his sides was Tim Mercer.

10

'Tim!' Sarah cried, feeling the rain lashing into her face. 'Sarah, I've got to see you,' Tim's voice was hoarse.

He looked dreadful, his eyes were hollow and had such an expression of fear in them. Sarah had never seen him like that, but she could only feel anger at him for disturbing her sleep. Swiftly she pushed the door, but Tim stopped her with his hand.

'Go away, Tim,' she begged him.

'It's about Alice.'

That pulled Sarah up sharp. 'Alice?' she repeated.

'Please, Sarah, let me in, I'm soaked to the skin.'

Believing fervently she would live to regret it, Sarah allowed Tim to enter the vestibule. He followed her upstairs and once in the living room, she switched on the electric fire because she could see he was shivering with cold. He held his hands out gratefully to the warming glow.

'What's this about Alice?' she pushed him, wanting him out of here as quickly as possible, despite the wretched weather outside. 'And how do you know her in the first place?'

'I'm Mark,' Tim stated simply.

Sarah sat down and Tim also sat, wiping the wet from his face and his hair as best he could with his hands. Before Sarah could speak, Tim went on, 'I gave her the wrong name, I didn't know how much she knew about me.'

'As far as I'm aware, Alice knew nothing at all about you.' She certainly hadn't mentioned him and was quite sure Gareth hadn't either.

Now that Tim had told her, Sarah realised she wasn't greatly surprised. She had had her suspicions in the first place, but no real grounds for them.

'So you called here when Gareth and I were out and made yourself known to Alice.'

'Yes. She was in the garden . . . '

'Spare me the details,' Sarah broke in, 'she's already told me. And you struck up a friendship with her. Why, Tim? To get back at me? At Gareth? Out of a weird sense of pleasure.'

'At first,' Tim didn't look at her. 'Later, the more I saw of her, the more I liked her and when she suggested she come and live with me, I didn't hesitate.'

Sarah stared at him. 'Alice suggested it?'

Sarah could see Alice's face, when she and Gareth announced their engagement. Her excitement. Not for them then, but for herself. She didn't doubt that Tim was telling her the truth.

'But none of this tells me why you turn up on my doorstep at three o'clock in the morning.'

'No.' Tim leaned forward and rested his face on his hands. This was a new Tim, dejected, short of something to say.

But could she trust him?

His words when he finally spoke were muffled. 'She's ill, Sarah and I don't know what to do. I'm scared.'

A cold hand clutched at Sarah's heart. 'How ill?'

'I don't know. She's been bad for a few days now. Hot. Feverish. Complaining of aches and pains. I wanted to bring her home but she wouldn't let me. Now . . . she's really bad. Burning up, whimpering all the time.'

'Have you called a doctor? Taken her to hospital?'

This wasn't what she thought it was she told herself. It couldn't be. Alice was too old, but Gareth had said the disease struck young adults as well as children. And in her weakened state of health it would make her more susceptible.

'No, I've done nothing,' Tim admitted, 'I didn't want you and her brother to know where she was.'

Sarah's anger flared. 'You fool! Don't you know she has a weak heart?'

'A weak heart?' Tim repeated.

169

Sarah could tell by the expression on his face that Alice hadn't thought to mention it to him.

'So where is she, Tim? At your house?'

'No. She's outside. In the car.'

Unable to say anything because she knew if she did she might start pummelling Tim with her fists, Sarah once again left the flat, rushing down the stairs and out into the still pouring rain. She saw Tim's car parked near the kerb and wrenched open the rear door. Thank goodness it wasn't locked.

★ ★ ★

Alice was lying on the back seat, wrapped in a blanket, her head on a couple of pillows. She was very still, very quiet and when Sarah reached inside and touched her face, she almost recoiled from the heat. Alice gave out a long, low moan.

Sarah turned to see Tim at her shoulders. 'I've got to get Gareth,' she

170

told him. 'I want you to wait upstairs, Tim. I know your basic instincts might be to flee but don't. Have a drink if you like, but wait.'

He seemed surprised by her suggestion that he might want to leave.

'Of course I'll wait,' he said and moved away.

Sarah dashed round the corner and up the drive of The White House. She went straight to the surgery door and pressed the lighted emergency button, keeping her finger on the buzzer.

It seemed an eternity before a light went on inside and there were sounds of the door being unlocked and a bolt being drawn. Then Gareth was there, in his dressing gown, tousled from sleep, but instantly alert when he saw Sarah.

Her first reaction when she saw his shocked expression was to burst into tears.

When Gareth brought her home from the hospital just as it was getting light, Sarah knew they had both to face Tim, provided he was still there, of course. She had a low opinion of him, but she couldn't stop herself thinking that, despite his promise, he might have fled into the night.

She turned to Gareth before they got out of the car. 'Well, he's still here,' she said, nodding towards Tim's Jaguar.

Gareth's face was grim. 'I don't know whether I can trust myself to face him, Sarah,' he murmured.

'I dislike him as much as you do, Gareth,' Sarah said, 'but we have to be fair, Alice went with him of her own free will.'

'I know. I know, but he should have taken her to hospital when she became ill. Why didn't he do that?'

'Perhaps if he'd known about her heart . . . ' Sarah couldn't believe she was defending Tim in this way.

'I've got to get back there. To the hospital. To be with her. They're not sure yet . . . about . . . I need to be there when they are.'

With the symptoms she was showing, Alice had been put straight into an isolation ward. Gareth had had to don cap and gown to be able to go in there. Sarah had had no choice but to wait in the waiting room until he came out.

'They keep telling me, assuring me that the epidemic is practically over,' he said when he re-appeared, looking tense, haggard, showing the signs of a seven o'clock shadow, 'but I've seen what that damned disease can do and what chance will Alice have?'

He started crying and Sarah caught him in her arms, holding him until he managed to control himself. He gave her a weak smile.

'Let's get you home,' he said.

At least, the rain had stopped.

Now there was another ordeal to face. Tim.

He was still sitting where Sarah had left him. There was no evidence that he had made himself a drink. He, too, looked unshaven and exhausted. He stood up when they came into the room.

'How is she?'

'We don't know. Only time will tell.' Gareth took a threatening step forwards and Sarah touched his arm.

'Gareth . . . ' she warned.

'It's all right. I'm not going to touch him.'

'I can only say I'm sorry, Dr Bradley,' Tim spoke humbly and he looked genuine enough. 'Alice was so full of life, how could I know about her? It all seemed to happen so quickly. I thought she just had a cold. People get colds all the time. They shake them off.'

'And you never even thought about poliomyelitis?' Gareth threw at him.

'No! Oh, I knew about the epidemic, sure I did. I can read the papers as much as the next man, but, Alice and I, we were living for the moment. Her words, not mine, that's how she wanted it. How could I know?' He slumped down into the chair again.

This all sounded so much like Alice, Sarah thought. She glanced at Gareth and she saw that he knew it too.

'I think you'd better go,' Gareth said.

'Can I contact you, to find out how she is?'

Sarah could see that Gareth was about to say no, so she beat him to it. 'There can't be any harm in that, Gareth.'

Gareth sighed. 'All right, but don't go to see her, not at the hospital, not here.'

'OK. I'll agree to that, but, later, when she's better, if she wants to see me . . . well, that's surely up to Alice.'

He walked towards the door, then turned. 'She's a wonderful girl, Dr Bradley.'

He really likes her, Sarah thought.

When they were alone, Gareth sat down and rested his head on the back of the sofa, closing his eyes.

'You need to get some sleep,' Sarah told him.

'And so do you. We've both been up half the night.'

He sat up straight again and held out his hand to Sarah. She took hold of it and went to sit beside him. 'If Alice pulls through . . . '

'When she pulls through,' Sarah said stoutly.

'Yes, of course, you're right, well, when she does I'm going to have to ease up on her a little. She always did say I fussed too much. She needs to go out more; she needs her own friends.

'No wonder she jumped at that Mercer fellow, keeping it a secret from me. Will you mind Alice living with us, Sarah? I know she can be a pain in the neck . . . '

Sarah had already prepared herself for sharing a home with Gareth's sister, and she hastened to reassure him.

'The White House was Alice's home before it was mine,' she smiled.

But she did nurture a dream that Alice, after tasting freedom, however briefly, might decide she wanted her own place. Somewhere close where she could be independent, make new friends, yet where they could keep their eye on her.

'I want Alice to be able to lead her

own life, if that's what she wants,' Gareth went on. 'She might become a better judge of people, not be taken in by someone like Tim Mercer.'

Sarah said nothing, but she couldn't help thinking that perhaps it was Tim who was taken in by Alice, in a way, and she never thought she would ever be able to think that about her former boyfriend.

When Gareth came round with news of Alice, Sarah could see the relief evident on his face.

'She hasn't got polio,' he announced. 'She did catch a cold and was exhausted, with a very high temperature, and her heartbeat was rather erratic for a while, but that's under control now. She's very weak, and she'll be in hospital for a few days yet and then she's going to have to take it easy, but she'll make our wedding, Sarah.'

'Thank God,' Sarah said fervently. 'Is she allowed any visitors?'

'Of course. And I've told her about Edith being here.'

'What did she say?' Sarah asked cautiously.

Gareth smiled. 'Well, she rolled her eyes heavenwards and sighed a great deal, but when I told her Edith and Audrey will be moving into their own place soon, Alice decided to be magnanimous about it. And by the way, she's apologised for what she did to Audrey. She knows she did wrong and she wants to be able to make it up to the child.'

Well, Sarah thought, that remains to be seen.

To Gareth she said, 'When can I see her?'

'Whenever you want.'

★   ★   ★

So they went that afternoon and joined the queue of other visitors to the wards. Alice had been moved into a small side room off a general ward. She was sitting up in bed wearing a fluffy pink bed jacket, looking surprisingly well with healthy colour in her cheeks.

'Sarah!' She held out her arms and Sarah went and embraced her.

'How are you feeling?' she asked.

'Wonderful! Especially now I've got my own room. The general ward was awful, I couldn't get a wink of sleep.' Her voice was slightly hoarse and heavy from her cold, but otherwise she seemed to be recovering well.

Sarah sat on the one available chair and Gareth stood by the window. 'You certainly look better than you did the other night.'

Alice lowered her eyes. 'I know. Poor Tim, he must have been so worried about me. I had no idea, of course, that you knew him, Sarah, or indeed that his name was Tim. That was naughty of him,' but she sounded more indulgent than cross. 'Anyway,' she smoothed her hands over the immaculate bedspread, 'I shan't be seeing him again. It was a mistake going away like that, and I'm sorry I upset you both.' Then she smiled, a wicked smile, 'But it was fun!'

Gareth came and took hold of her wrist in a doctor-like gesture and Sarah knew that, unethically, he was checking Alice's pulse, but she submitted to him without protest.

'And we wouldn't want to stop you having fun, would we, Sarah?' Gareth said.

'How kind of you!' Alice gave her brother a sweet smile. To Sarah she said, 'May I be a bridesmaid, Sarah? I presume you've already asked Audrey.'

Sarah nodded. 'Yes, I have and yes, you may.'

'Thank you.'

Alice was being especially gracious. She was coming across as the sweet young thing who was sorry for causing so much trouble and was promising not to do it again.

'Tell me all about the wedding,' she begged. 'And, of course, I haven't seen your ring,' she grabbed hold of Alice's left hand unceremoniously, studying the solitaire diamond in great detail. 'It's lovely,' she breathed. 'Oh, Sarah, do you think I'll ever get married? Oh, not to someone like Tim Mercer,' she gave a little shudder which effectively consigned Tim to history, 'but someday, to somebody nice who will look after me.'

Heaven help him, Sarah thought. 'I'm sure you will, Alice,' but Sarah wished she could cross her fingers as she said this.

She and Gareth left soon afterwards. Alice seemed to tire and leaned back on her mound of pillows, closing her eyes. Gareth bent over her, kissing her pale forehead.

'We'll see you tomorrow,' he said softly.

Briefly Alice opened her eyes. 'Yes, I'll look forward to that.'

Gareth stopped to have a brief word with Alice's doctor, then joined Sarah as they left the hospital and walked to the car park. He was whistling.

'My sister is tougher than I thought,' he admitted, taking hold of Sarah's hand.

'I think she certainly has a strong character,' Sarah agreed.

Gareth laughed. 'Very diplomatically put, darling. Well now, after all the drama, do you think we can start to look forward to our wedding?'

'I'm sure we can.'

The weather had started to brighten up after the storm and Sarah had a real hope that it might be kind to them on October the 15th. She didn't think they would see Tim again, she felt sure he had learned his lesson and would, if not completely change his ways, at least be humbled by his experience with Alice.

Edith and Audrey would move into their little cottage and be a family again. As for Alice . . . well, she would always be Alice. Lovable, exasperating, irritating, someone you could cheerfully shake one moment, and fold in your arms the next.

And Sarah and Gareth? They would get married and Sarah would probably be known for evermore as 'the doctor's wife' but that was something she wouldn't mind in the least.

We do hope that you have enjoyed reading this large print book.

Did you know that all of our titles are available for purchase?

We publish a wide range of high quality large print books including:
Romances, Mysteries, Classics
General Fiction
Non Fiction and Westerns

Special interest titles available in large print are:
The Little Oxford Dictionary
Music Book, Song Book
Hymn Book, Service Book

Also available from us courtesy of Oxford University Press:
Young Readers' Dictionary
(large print edition)
Young Readers' Thesaurus
(large print edition)

For further information or a free brochure, please contact us at:
Ulverscroft Large Print Books Ltd.,
The Green, Bradgate Road, Anstey,
Leicester, LE7 7FU, England.
Tel: (00 44) **0116 236 4325**
Fax: (00 44) **0116 234 0205**

THE EAGLE STONE

Heather Pardoe

While assisting her father in selling provisions to visitors to the top of Snowdon, Elinor Owen meets the adventuress Lady Sara Raglan and her handsome nephew, Richard. Eli is swiftly drawn into Lady Sara's most recent adventure, becoming a spy for Queen Victoria's government. Now, up against the evil Jacques, Eli and Richard are soon fighting for their lives, while Lady Sara heads for a final showdown and pistols at dawn with Jacques on the summit of Snowdon itself.